Katie John and
Heathcliff

Katie John and Heathcliff

by Mary Calhoun

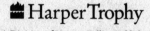

HarperTrophy
A Division of HarperCollins*Publishers*

To Kathy, who asked for this book,
and to Katie, who is named for Katie John

KATIE JOHN AND HEATHCLIFF
Copyright © 1980 by Mary H. Wilkins
All rights reserved. No part of this book may be used or reproduced in any manner whatsoever without written permission except in the case of brief quotations embodied in critical articles and reviews. Printed in the United States of America. For information address HarperCollins Children's Books, a division of HarperCollins Publishers, 10 East 53rd Street, New York, N.Y. 10022.

First Harper Trophy edition, 1981.

Library of Congress Cataloging in Publication Data
Calhoun, Mary.
   Katie John and Heathcliff.

   SUMMARY: Former boy-hater Katie John falls in
love for the first time.
   I. Title.
PZ7.C1278Kav   [Fic]   80-7770
ISBN 0-06-020931-3
ISBN 0-06-020932-1 (lib. bdg.)
ISBN 0-06-440120-0 (pbk.)

Contents

1

Looking for Heathcliff

That August before seventh grade Katie John read *Jane Eyre.* Then she read *Wuthering Heights.* Then she tried a couple of paperbacks that had lurid covers and passionate titles. However, the male heroes in those books were cold oatmeal compared to Heathcliff. He was so fierce, yet so compellingly romantic, boy and man. Katie went back to *Wuthering Heights* and read again the early and ending parts about Heathcliff and Catherine Earnshaw. . . . Dark Heathcliff at the window calling into the storm for his dead love, "Come in, Cathy! Oh, my heart's darling, hear me *this* time, Catherine, at last!"

Katie shivered. That was *her* name. *Katherine! Oh, Kathy! Oh—* Oh, nonsense! Katie John

1

slammed the book down.

Going to a new school, Junior High—that was the excitement to think about.

The first day, of course, she walked with Sue Halsey, who lived just down the block and who was her best friend. Dear plump Sue always knew the right thing to do at the right time. That could be maddening, yet a comfort, when starting at an unknown school.

"A new school! New teachers! New kids!" Katie chanted. "A new start!"

"Um," agreed Sue. "Did you see Don Cordova on TV last night? He was singing 'Tonight Is the Night,' and—oh!"

"Oh—junk!" Katie John exclaimed. Don Cordova was junk compared to Heathcliff.

"He is not!" Sue declared. "Don Cordova is marvelous! Who do you know that's more—you know—wonderful?"

Katie didn't answer. She wondered what Heathcliff's hands were like. Did the book say? Hairy? Smooth and fine? Dark, strong? Katie John's stomach queased. The passion of Heathcliff and Catherine was almost too much for her.

She fixed her attention outward on the fine old houses they were passing, while she answered "Um" to Sue's chatter. Going to Junior High meant walking a different route through a neighborhood of mansions in varying degrees of grandeur and decay. Each was set in gracious lawns, some bounded by wrought-iron fences. Barton's Bluff, Missouri, was a Mississippi River town, and its hilly streets were lined with houses built in Civil War times or later in the nineteenth century.

A squarish brick place had impressive white stonework going up its corners, but its mansard roof looked dinky, Katie thought, compared to the generous way the roof folded down over the top of her own house. Across the street, a house looked empty, with no curtains at the blank windows, and the carved wooden balcony was breaking away—maybe a good place to explore on Halloween. Now the next house, built of yellow sandstone blocks—she liked the rich warm look of it in the September sunshine. For a moment Katie wished her house had been built of golden stone instead of red brick.

But no, then it wouldn't be the house she loved.

Katie John had lived only two years and a summer in the one-hundred-year-old house her great-grandfather had built. When Great-Aunt Emily Clark had died and Mother inherited the house, the Tuckers had come from California intending to sell the property. Katie had thought the big brick house was ugly—until she began to explore the house's secrets. By the end of that summer, by the time Dad had repaired the place to saleable condition, the Tuckers couldn't bear to leave the dear old house and Barton's Bluff.

Of course, she would always love her house the best, Katie thought; but each of the old homes along

3

the street had something special about it to notice. On the next corner, a tall thin brick house was ordinary, except that it was guarded by two life-sized stone dogs. They crouched on either side of steps that led up from the sidewalk to the lawn. Katie John studied the smooth gray stone dogs. Such lean, noble dogs, their ears alert . . . Were they greyhounds?

"Wait a sec," she told Sue.

Katie ran up the steps and touched the sun-warmed stone of a dog. She saw the tip of his left ear was chipped off. And his back sank down more than it should have. She looked at the other dog. Both stone dogs were swaybacked.

"You know what?" she called to Sue. "I'll bet these dogs are worn down from generations of children sitting on them."

"Um-hm. Come on."

"Wait, let me try—"

Katie John straddled the chip-eared dog, and her bottom settled comfortably in the depression on his back. A child could lean forward on the reared neck, arms around the warm stone. . . . *Good dog.* She liked the thought of all those little boys and girls sitting on the dogs, maybe having pretend races or dreaming a flight into the sky on a lean greyhound . . . children long grown up and gone. . . .

"Hey, kid! Get offa that dog!"

The shout came from a man pushing a lawn mower around the side of the house.

4

As Katie John hastily slid off the dog, she saw two boys go by on the sidewalk. Of course, they were staring at her. One of the boys had strangely pale eyes, considering his shaggy black hair. Walking on, the other boy said something quick and laughed. The black-haired boy looked back at Katie again, but he didn't laugh, only looked at her.

Maybe Heathcliff had looked at Catherine that way, an intense, measuring look. Goodness, was her stomach churning like this just because a boy had looked at her? Ah, probably he was only wondering why a big girl—twelve and a half!—was playing on the dog like a baby.

"Honestly, Katie John!" Sue exclaimed. "Aren't you ever going to grow up?"

"Certainly," Katie replied with dignity. "I'm already halfway there. Who are those boys?" They were a block ahead by now, walking with longer strides.

Sue shrugged. "I don't know. Probably some eighth graders."

There were plenty of new faces to see, when they got to school. Not only did the Junior High take in eighth and ninth grades, but there were three elementary schools to pour in seventh graders. In front of the brick building that long ago had been the Senior High, four school buses unloaded flows of kids. Boys tossed a football at one side of the school; girls darted from group to group on the grass; people lounged on the broad steps. It was a swarm of

5

strangers, all jigging with electricity, ready for something new after the long hot summer.

A lot of the boys looked older than the ones Katie was used to looking at. Even the boys she knew from sixth grade looked older. There was Howard Bunch, big and noisy, tossing a ball with quick little Sammy, Pete Hallstrom—who was going to be tall as a tree, if he didn't quit growing—and Bob, who had been Sue's friend forever.

"Hey, Katie John!" the boys called. "Hey, Sue!"

"Hey," Katie John responded rather moodily, as she watched Howard grab good-natured Bob by the shoulders and wrestle him to the ground. The boys might look older, but they acted just as kiddish as ever.

At first, when Katie saw Edwin Jones coming up the sidewalk, he seemed different. His face had grown longer, so that he looked almost distinguished, with his thin nose and high forehead. Early in the summer, she and Edwin had had a fine time helping an archeology team excavate Indian relics Edwin had found. But she hadn't seen him since mid-July, when he'd gone deep down in Missouri to help on his uncle's farm.

For a moment Katie John wondered if Edwin might be something like Heathcliff. Edwin was strong-minded, and he could keep long silences when she didn't know what he was thinking. Like Heathcliff and Catherine roaming the English moors, she and Edwin explored the hills above the

6

Mississippi River.

"Say, Katie," he said, hurrying up to her, "do you know anything about geodes?"

His voice squeaked, and his hair was just as yellow duck–feathery as ever. Katie John snorted at herself. Edwin couldn't be a Heathcliff. She knew him too well.

Still, Edwin's new project sounded like fun.

"Listen, you know that creek that runs through the cemetery? Well, I found two geodes in the creek bed now it's dry, and I bet if we dig around, we can find a bunch more."

"All I know about geodes is they're beautiful inside."

On the outside they were dull-looking round gray stones, but cracked open, the hollow insides were lined with sparkling crystals. Katie had seen geodes cemented to the steps of old houses or lining the front walks.

"Hey, yeah!" she added. "I could collect geodes to line our front walk."

"Well—I guess you could. I was thinking of cracking and selling them. They're rare enough, Katie— they're worth good money, you know."

Always down-to-earth, Edwin was. And why not? Katie thought, amused. Edwin lived in the cemetery, where his father was the caretaker.

A deafening bell rang to summon everyone inside, and that was the beginning of the Noise. The old school building, with its high ceilings, bare

7

wooden floors, and hallways lined with metal lockers, was the clatteriest place Katie John had ever been. Wait till all those lockers began banging! Feet rumbled on the floors, and chatter and laughter bounced off the walls, as the kids, nearly three hundred of them, thronged toward the auditorium for the opening assembly. Katie John stuck her fingers in her ears, then hastily took them out when she saw a sleek-looking girl staring at her.

It was a rackety old auditorium, too. The sound of three hundred kids talking all at once in an echoing cavern was awesome. Signs—SEVENTH, EIGHTH and NINTH—sorted the students into the three sections of seats. As Katie and Sue edged into a row containing some girls from their sixth grade, Katie John felt a sudden pang of nerves. How could she get along in a new school with All These People?

Looking over the mass of faces, she saw Sue had had those boys pegged right. The shaggy-haired, light-eyed boy was sitting in the eighth-grade section. He was talking to a girl. Katie John sniffed and concentrated on the rows of teacher faces on the stage in front.

When the introductions had been made and schedules passed out, she began to feel confident again. English, her best-loved subject, came first thing in the morning, when she was ready for new ideas. And, upon comparing schedules with Sue, she found they shared some of the classes: English, Gym and Homemaking.

"Homemaking—ugh!" Katie John exclaimed. "I wanted to take Shop, so I could learn to repair things and help Dad around the house."

In the old house there was always something that needed fixing.

"You can do that next year. This year," Sue teased, "you can learn how to help your mother in the kitchen."

"Sure, she'll love that! Well, at least we'll have cooking class last thing in the morning, when our stomachs are looking for lunch."

Some benevolent soul in the school office had made it possible for the seventh-grade girls to meet the eighth-grade boys by arranging the schedule so that half the seventh and eighth graders had classes in Shop, and the other half in Homemaking. When Katie John arrived at the Home lab, she saw the shaggy-haired boy eyeing a stove as if it were a strange animal. Katie John's heart gave a thump. Cooking class might not be so dull, after all.

Howard Bunch was in the class, too. He was loudly declaring, "I already know how to fry eggs. That's all anybody needs to know!"

The teacher, Mrs. Bartlett, even looked like a homemaker. She had a pretty, dimpled face and a sprightly air about her.

"Future homemakers, welcome!" she said. "You'll learn to cook and sew, and when we get to the family unit, we'll borrow a baby from somewhere, and you can learn to change diapers and cuddle and burp. First, though, you'll have to practice on a doll."

The boys whooped at the idea of burping a doll. A training class for baby-sitters, Katie thought, smiling. She saw the light-eyed boy returning her smile, not whooping like the other boys.

Mrs. Bartlett divided the class into teams of four: head cook, first assistant, second assistant and housekeeper (cleaner-upper). Jobs on the team would rotate every time they cooked something. And lo, the shaggy-headed boy was on Katie's team, and his name was Jason Schreiber. The reason his eyes looked so startling, she decided, was that they were speckled, and the blueness was emphasized by heavy dark eyelashes.

When Katie John came to attention again, Mrs. Bartlett was saying "—table manners and nutrition. And so, we'll start off by making crab-apple jelly tomorrow. Today we'll go out and pick the crab apples."

"All right!" was the cry at the prospect of being out of school again so soon.

In the swarm for the doorway, Jason Schreiber was beside Katie John, speaking to her, saying, "I can never be head cook. You'll have to show me how to use that stove."

"Me!" Katie John exclaimed. "I don't know anything about cooking."

That could have been the wrong thing to say, for Jason didn't reply but hurried forward to catch up with a boy. It was the truth, though. If, in an emergency, her mother called upon her to fix dinner, it had to be meat loaf and baked potatoes, because that was all Katie knew how to cook.

The class trooped noisily in the sunshine toward the fruit trees two blocks away in Mrs. Bartlett's friend's yard. Everyone had a brown paper sack to fill with crab apples. Howard Bunch and some of the boys pulled the sacks over their heads and stumbled down the sidewalk, boisterous blind men. Katie John was about to clown with her sack on her head, too, but then she looked at Jason Schreiber, and she didn't. Instead of horsing around like the seventh-grade boys, he slouched along with his fingertips stuck in his back jeans pockets, listening to some guy talk.

The trees were studded with the little red apples, and at first a few of the apples went into the paper sacks. But Sammy tossed one at Howard, and Howard socked a crab apple back at Sammy's belly button—"Catch!" Then hard red pellets whizzed through the air. One hit Katie on the shoulder. Howard had thrown it, so she burned an apple back at him—"One for you, too, fella!" It caught Howard square in the chest, and it happened that that crab apple was extra ripe. It squished.

"Ha ha!" Katie roared. She saw that Jason boy looking at her and sobered, and while she was off guard, Sammy landed a crab apple on her hip. "Ow!"

11

Mrs. Bartlett called into the crab-apple melee, "First one to fill a sack gets an *A* in apple-picking!" Red pellets continued to fly, so she added, shouting, "Last one to fill a sack gets to scrub all the stoves after we cook the jelly."

Plunkings of apples into sacks began in earnest then. As Katie John bent to pick up crab apples tossed on the ground, a voice teased behind her.

"I know how you got your pants dirty." It was Jason.

Katie became aware of her rump up and she straightened. "Huh?" Nothing wrong with her front. She craned to look at her back. The seat of her pants was black. In honor of the first day of school she had worn her best white pants, but now the back of them was smudgy black. The hollow on that stone dog must have been grimy with the coal dust that covered everything outdoors in Barton's Bluff. Katie John whacked her hand at her seat, but she'd sat on the dirt too long through the morning for it to dust away.

"Oh, sheee!" she sighed. Here she'd thought she looked okay on the first morning of Junior High, when all the time everybody had been looking at her grimy bottom. "Oh, grunge!"

" 'Sall right. Adds character." Jason smiled at her. "What were you doing on that dog?"

Imagining. Could she say that to this boy?

"Checking out the speed of a greyhound," Katie John said flippantly.

12

"Huh, yeah!" Smiling and shaking his head, Jason reached for more crab apples.

So it was an okay thing to say. Still, she felt uneasy about the flippancy. Oh, why on earth should she care what Jason Schreiber thought?

Yet, during the week, like one possessed, Katie John kept noticing other new boys. In Math, when a boy named George went up to the blackboard to demonstrate working a problem, she liked how lean and fine his hands were. She found out he'd gone to Pumphrey, the rich kids' grade school. When a dark-haired boy named Ramon picked up a notebook she'd dropped by her locker, she was touched by his gallantry. They talked for a few minutes, and he told her his father, a new doctor in town, was from the Philippines.

"But I was born in Ba-a-aston," he added, and then she was intrigued by his Boston accent.

That night she thought how liquid-brown Ramon's eyes were.

She caught herself up. *Why are you thinking about boys? That way. Stop it!*

The next day in English, when a boy named Scott said, "That's stupid," Katie was fascinated with the way he said *stew-pid*. He had a square, ugly face, and the corners of his mouth went into a wry smile when he persisted, "No, that's stew-pid." It sounded so sophisticated. She wanted to hear him say it again.

Talking, turning his head, he caught her eye and saw her staring at him. Katie John looked away in shame. Honestly! What was the matter with her? Just last year she'd organized a Boy-Haters' club. Now it was "here a boy, there a boy, everywhere a boy-boy!"

Firmly she told herself, You are not going to get silly about boys! Staunchly, for the rest of the day, she kept her mind on her lessons.

The last thing that afternoon—it was Thursday— Ramon came up to her by her locker.

"Look," he said, "some of us are going to the movies tomorrow night. You want to go? I'll pay your way."

Katie's throat went tight, and her face felt prickly. She stuck her head inside the locker, as if she were looking for something, so her face wouldn't show. A boy was asking her for a date, and she didn't know what to do. She hadn't expected it. It wasn't like Edwin saying "Let's go hunt geodes in the creek."

Stalling, she muttered, "What's on at the show?" She couldn't keep her head in the locker. She looked at Ramon and was extremely aware of his brown eyes.

"Hot Car, Slow Lady," he said, smiling.

"Oh. Well. Well, I hate car-chase movies. So I guess I'd better not go."

It was the truth, but Ramon just stood there looking kind of nervous.

So Katie added feebly, "All that screeching of

14

tires and noise—you know. I'm sorry. Maybe some other time."

"Yeah, okay." He nodded, smiling again, and walked away.

Katie John let out a big sigh, whether of relief or frustration she didn't know. She closed her locker door and found that her hands were trembling the way they had one time after a car had almost run over her.

2

Fly Away with Me

Then on Friday a balloon blossomed over Barton's Bluff, and a new enchantment took possession of Katie John. She was a little late for school that morning, running by herself, when the balloon drifted into sight over the treetops. Like a fantasy in the sky, suddenly there was the great billowing of red, blue and green just above her. It was so low she could even see the people riding in the basket below the balloon.

Downtown Katie had noticed the posters saying that hot-air balloon rides would be available at the Street Fair that weekend, and she'd been mildly interested. Now, seeing the glorious blossom in the air, its gentle drifting motion, Katie felt a surging desire: The Balloon! The Balloon! She had to go up

16

in the Balloon!

Edwin was hurrying up the school steps when she got there.

"Edwin!" she called.

At the same time, the balloon appeared again, higher in the sky. Edwin and Katie John stood still and watched the great bubble sail noiselessly over the town toward the river.

"We've got to go up in the balloon!" Katie John exclaimed. "Edwin, go with me! It'll be our best adventure yet."

"Can't." He shook his head. "Poster says it costs twenty dollars."

Edwin had earned money working on his uncle's farm in the summer, but he'd spent it on school clothes and the subscription to his archeology magazine. Katie had enough money saved—just barely.

"Oh, Edwin!" she wailed. "I've just got to go! But—" For over a year they had adventured and explored together. It wasn't fair for her to go up in the balloon, if Edwin couldn't afford to. "I won't go, if you can't."

"No, Katie John, you do it," Edwin said, his long face solemn. "After all, I got to explore a cave on my uncle's farm, and you missed that."

"All right," she said at once, guiltily, happily.

She felt a little more guilty when she remembered she'd promised Edwin to go geode hunting on Saturday. But they could do that anytime.

There was no question of Sue going up in the

17

balloon with Katie John. Sue wouldn't even go up on a Ferris wheel. For a while there was some question about Katie's going, for her mother wondered about the danger. However, with Dad's jovial assistance, at last she begged a signed permission sheet from her mother.

Saturday morning, running down the steep hill from her house to the riverfront with Sue, Katie John was inspired to paraphrase Robert Louis Stevenson. She sang out,

> "How would you like to go up in a balloon,
> Up in the air so high?
> Oh, I do think it the loveliest thing
> To drift away in the sky!"

"Yes, and maybe not come back in one piece," Sue muttered.

In past Septembers the Street Fair had extended the length of Main Street for a week. This year the Fair was spread out down on the waterfront levee and only for the weekend. A lot of the kids planned to go to the Fair that night, but there were plenty of families in from the country, and the Fair was going full tilt first thing in the morning. Down there by the Mississippi, the girls beheld an exciting noisy conglomeration of rides whirling, lights flashing, music blaring and barkers calling at the "win-a-prize" games.

But when the girls entered the hubbub of the Fair, they found it did not contain the joys of last year. There was no crazy house, no Gypsy fortune-teller, no high-wire walker or trapeze act, not even a sideshow with the fat lady and the dog-faced boy. It was just a tawdry carnival.

"And where's the balloon?" Katie John demanded. She'd expected to see it tethered, hanging in the air over the Fair.

"Maybe it's off killing somebody," Sue grumped.

"Oh, Sue!"

"Look at that darling stuffed bear!" Sue pointed to a prize at a ring-toss game. "I want to try for him."

"Punk-robber game," Katie said scornfully. "If you want to waste your money on that, do it while I'm up in the balloon. Come on."

As they passed the crack of rifles at moving metal ducks, Katie caught a glimpse of red and blue. Beyond a cluster of people, the mass of balloon cloth lay crumpled on the ground. Maybe it had burst! Katie John pushed through the people, and then she found out that no, the balloon was all right. That was just the way it started out. Near it was the inflator fan, and the basket sat upright, inviting riders.

A young man wearing little nose glasses, who seemed to be the proprietor of the balloon, was saying to an onlooker, "Let's go now! The air's just right." He looked intellectual with those glasses, but he talked slangy. "Make up your mind, Jack, if you wanta fire-fly."

Katie John looked at the crumpled balloon. A scorched spot showed near the mouth of the cloth.

Up close, it didn't look a fantasy at all, but just a flashy bunch of rather dirty nylon. Was everything this morning to be a disappointment? But the air . . . being up in the air, drifting . . .

"Here"—she held out her money and the permission sheet to the nose-glasses fellow—"I want to go."

"I'm the pilot. Give it to them." He indicated a bearded young man and wiry girl lounging against a pickup truck. "Okay, that makes four passengers, and we need a fifth. How about you?" he said to Sue. "C'mon, babe, let's fly."

Sue looked flustered and shook her head.

"Ah, Sue, do come," urged Katie. "It'll be like—like a flying carpet."

"No!" Sue had her lower lip set. "Anyway," she said with relief, "I don't have enough money."

A boy stepped out of the cluster of people. "Look, if we don't go pretty soon, I want my money back." He was Jason Schreiber.

Katie John became very still. Was she going to fly up in the balloon with Jason? What would that mean?

Maybe not much. Because a girl stepped up beside him, saying, "Yes, I'm tired of waiting." She was the sleek-looking girl who had stared at Katie that first day of school, when Katie had stuck her fingers in her ears against all the noise. The girl seemed so self-possessed she could have been a ninth grader, but she was in the seventh grade, because she was in Katie's Gym class. Her name was Trish Hard-wicke.

Now why should her heart thump, just because Jason was on a balloon date with Trish?

But maybe it wasn't quite that way. Another boy stepped out of the crowd, saying, "Yeah, come on, Trish. We can find plenty else to do." He was Jason's friend who had seen Katie on the stone dog.

"Like what, Chuck?" Jason said. "Anyway, young Katie here wants to go."

He nodded to her, smiling slightly, and she didn't know how he meant that "young Katie" business.

"Anybody else?" the bearded man asked the on-lookers. When no one spoke up, he told the pilot, "You'd better go, before the day gets too warm. So, we take a low-profit trip. Come on, passengers, give us a hand."

He and the pilot picked up edges of the nylon envelope, while the girl aimed the inflator fan into the cavity. Katie went forward with the others to help hold up the mouth of the balloon so the air could fill it, and it was fun to be part of the crew scrambling to get the balloon ready. When she peered inside the lifting cloth, the cavity looked as colorful as a circus arena.

Jason isn't particularly with *her*, Katie John told herself. They're just all three together.

"I can hardly wait!" she exclaimed to Jason.

"Beats walking."

He was so sophisticated!

Gradually the balloon billowed into the air, and once inflated it was a fantasy, after all. It bloomed just above the basket, tethered by ropes which the bearded man and the girl held, and Katie John and the others climbed into the gondola. The pilot was busy adjusting the overhead burner, which was connected to one of several propane tanks inside the basket.

Katie asked him, "Don't the rest of your crew get to go up?"

"Sure. We just do this—give rides—to pay for our flights. Costs plenty to buy a balloon, fly a balloon."

Katie John was glad a fifth passenger hadn't come. It was crowded enough in the basket. And then she forgot everybody, because the ground began to fall away. The man and the girl were below, letting go of the ropes. Out of the crowd, Sue's face looked up, fearful, trying to smile. Up over the hurly-burly of the carnival they rose, above the Ferris wheel. . . . The amazing thing was that there was almost no sensation of movement, no sudden whoosh upward, but simply the earth dropping away.

It was not a silent lift-off. The pilot did something to the burner; it roared, and flame shot up into the balloon. No wonder the cloth was singed, Katie thought, looking up into the bright bubble.

She looked over the side of the basket. How high up they were already!

"There's my house!" she exclaimed.

From above, it was a brick island cradled in tall trees, the flat roof and four chimneys the most apparent. How marvelous to see the house from this angle! Katie John realized she must be the only one of four generations of family to see the house from the air.

"Where?" Jason was beside her.

She pointed. "That brick house at the top of Second Street Hill."

"Some big house!"

Trish claimed his attention. "Jason, I can see your house. Yours too, Chuck."

"Can you see yours?" Katie asked her.

"Oh no, it's way out by the Country Club." Trish added to Jason, "And you know how all the oak trees hide it, anyway." She gave Katie a cool glance, then smiled from one boy to the other, saying lightly, "Too bad we couldn't get more of our crowd to come."

Katie John knew a put-down when it happened. Trish's clothes were just right. Her hair was just right. Katie felt a loathing for Trish Hardwicke.

But no, she wasn't going to let that girl spoil the balloon flight. Katie John looked up into the misty blueness of the air. She looked down through the haze, and she felt as if she were simply standing high in the air above everything, with not even enough wind of movement to ruffle her hair. Lightly, gently, they floated upriver. They were so high it was like being a bird to see the river winding between the hills, and then the high fields spreading back on each side of it as it got smaller and less important in the landscape.

Jason leaned out, looking, and Katie John became very aware of how close he was to her. They had to keep to one side of the basket and Trish and Chuck to the other to make a little path for the pilot. From time to time he squeezed back and forth between them from the burner to a cord that opened a panel at the top of the balloon. Whenever the pilot moved, Jason had to push up against Katie. He was a head taller than she was, she realized.

"What are you doing?" Jason asked the pilot between roaring blasts of the burner.

"Keeping the right amount of hot air in the envelope to maintain level flight. When we start to climb too high, I pull the rip cord to the parachute top and spill some air."

"How high are we?" Chuck asked.

The pilot pointed to an altimeter set in the side of the basket. "Three thousand feet."

"Wow! Say, can you control this so we land right back at the Street Fair?"

No, the man told Chuck, the other two would follow them with the chase truck.

Chuck said, "Trish, are you scared?" Playfully he took her hand.

She pulled back her hand. "Heavens, no!" And to the pilot, "I just wish I could take lessons to fly a balloon."

"Hundred dollars an hour, chick," he told her. "Sure, we could stay around awhile, if enough people wanted lessons."

Trish shook her long sleek hair. "Oh, I guess not. If I did that, I might have to give up my ski vacation at Aspen this Christmas."

Oh my, wouldn't that just be terrible, Katie thought, while the burner roared.

She'd heard about the country-club kids. They all played golf, swam in competition, rode horses in the Saddle Club shows, and now it seemed they enjoyed ski vacations at top-name resorts. At least Trish—

"*Sshish!*" Katie sighed.

Below, tiny, a towboat pushed a long pencil of barges up the river.

"Shall we say hello to the boat?" the pilot said.

He pulled the cord to the rip panel, and gradually the tow and the Mississippi grew larger until Katie could see the scallops of waves. She sucked in her breath in delight. There was no sensation of falling, only the feeling of drifting easily down the air.

But Trish exclaimed, "Oh, my goodness!"

She jerked back from the edge of the basket, her face tense, eyes looking away from the descent. Katie John was meanly glad, then ashamed.

When the basket dipped low enough to see men waving from the back deck of the towboat, the boat's horn sounded a loud toot of salute.

"Now, how about a little splash-and-dash, kids?"

The breezy-talking pilot was giving them a good ride for their money.

"What? Ohh!" Trish shrieked, as the balloon cruised lower over the river.

The basket touched the water, the burner roared, and the balloon sailed up into the air again.

"Whee!" Katie exclaimed. It was even better than the dip and rise of the Ferris wheel. "Wow!"

Jason said, "You're all right, Katie John."

Trish said quickly, "How exciting!"

"Wanta do it again?" The pilot moved to the rip cord.

"Yes! But—" Katie saw Trish was gripping the edge of the basket. "No, let's not." It was mean to put Trish through that again, if it really scared her.

However, the balloon was already coasting down toward the water. And Trish made a dear-little-girl act of being scared. She reached across to Jason, saying in a sweet trembly voice, "Hold my hand, Jason."

He shrugged, grinning, and took her hand.

Grunge! Katie John concentrated on the splashdown, as the basket touched the water far ahead of the towboat.

"Excuse me." Moving to fire the burner, the pilot broke up the handclasp.

Katie John stole a peek at Jason, and he didn't seem to care whether he held hands with Trish. His head was raised, looking up the river. Katie took a big breath and relaxed.

26

The basket lifted higher and higher, and there was no chance to talk over the noise of the burner. Katie John didn't want to anyway, for she was absorbed in the high, open flying. They were sailing over the wooded hills of Illinois above mounds of green treetops with bits of golden fields between. Here and there, spiking up through the trees, were church spires and water towers of little towns. They were drifting far, far away, Katie dreamed, on and on, and the chase truck would never catch them and make them come back. Floating free.

She looked at Jason and saw his face looked as dreamy as she felt. The burner stopped roaring, the balloon drifted, and there was the stillness of sharing, side by side.

"Have you ever," she murmured, "have you ever had such a wonderful free feeling in all your life?"

He looked at her with those light eyes. Were the speckles brown or gray?

"Never have." His gaze was intent, then he looked out over the panorama again, half smiling.

It was the way he looked at her. Katie recognized it then: Jason Schreiber was the one who could be a Heathcliff.

3

Somebody Wonderful

Just because Jason reminded her of Heathcliff, Katie
John told herself over the weekend, that didn't
mean she—she *liked* him. And even if she did—
kind of—it was only from a distance, as an observer.
And she certainly wasn't going to tell Sue or anybody about it. She wasn't going to be like Priscilla
and Betsy Ann and the other girls who even in sixth
grade had always been talking about boys and chas-
ing them.

So Monday morning, walking to school, Katie
John said to Sue, "Do you think Jason Schreiber is—
um—*smoky*?"

She'd been trying to think of a word for Jason.
Special? But a guy with three eyes would be special!
Romantically attractive? That sounded mucky. So-

phisticated? . . . Smoky. Maybe. Not really smoke, but like smouldering unknown things deep in him. And the way he looked.

"Huh? Smoky?" Sue was bewildered.

"I mean, like Humphrey Bogart is smoky."

Recently the girls had watched an old Bogart movie on television and had been entranced.

"Ohh. Smoky," Sue said thoughtfully. "Yeah. He is."

"Jason?"

"No. Bogart."

They stepped off one curb and up on the other while they thought about Bogart.

Sue said, "There's another guy—he's not exactly smoky, but you know who I think is somebody wonderful? Ronnie Hargrove." She ducked her head, giggling a little.

"Huh!" All Katie John had noticed about Ronnie was his pimples. However, something told her to indulge Sue. "Somebody Wonderful—*S.W.* Who else do you think is S.W.?"

"Mr. Carruthers," Sue said promptly.

"Good gosh, Sue! He's a grown man! Married!"

Mr. Carruthers was the pale, intense art teacher.

"Well, goodness, Katie John. I don't expect him to like *me.* I thought we were talking about—well— romantical guys. We aren't talking about—you know—getting *involved*, are we?"

"No, of course not." Katie John sincerely hoped somebody someday would call her his "heart's darling." But not yet, of course. "But what about Bob?"

"Why, sure, I like Bob the best for every day. But Bob isn't S.W. or smoky."

No. Katie grinned, thinking of Bob with his absolutely open, good ways and his head round as an apple.

Sue was laughing and looking at Katie. "Katie John! You never used to talk about boys. What happened with you and Jason up in that balloon?"

"Nothing! Look"—Katie changed the subject—"are you going to the cheerleader tryouts Friday?"

Four girls each from seventh and eighth grades were to be chosen as cheerleaders for the Junior Varsity football team. The football guys would vote on which cheerleaders they wanted.

"No," Sue said. "I'm not good at all that jumping around. And anyway, it's a dumb way to pick cheerleaders. It's just a popularity contest. I'm not sure enough boys would vote for me."

Katie John wasn't sure she wanted to test that, either. Yet it would be fun going to the games. Jason played football.

"Me either," Katie agreed, "but I'm going to try, anyway."

When she got to the Homemaking class that morning, Jason was sitting at a table, and she sat down opposite him. He didn't seem to notice her. He was studying a cookbook, and Katie recalled they were to have a quiz that day on measures. How many tablespoons to a cup? she tried to remember.

"Hi, balloon buddy," she said. Ugh, that sounded so hearty.

"Hi." He glanced up and nodded.

"Yeah, I heard you guys went up in the balloon," said another boy at the table. "How was it?"

"Oh, it was wonderful!"

"We didn't travel very far," Jason said. "It was like standing up in the air above everything."

Katie John had thought that, too, yet the way Jason said it, the experience didn't sound so great. Maybe he hadn't felt any of the things she had . . . the sharing. . . . She looked at Jason, but his head was bent over the cookbook again, so she reached for another book to study the weights-and-measures table.

Still, there was something about him—like, right then, the manly way he pressed his lips together as he studied the cookbook—she couldn't help admiring. At a distance, of course.

After school, Katie John practiced cheerleading. When she got home, she went right out to the back yard, where it was private and nobody could see. The broad brick house rose four stories high back there; a board fence shielded the yard from the sidewalk; brick carriage houses—"the barns"—bounded the alley side; and on the fourth side the vegetable gardens and fruit trees stretched away for half a block. Practicing leaps and splits, Katie chanted the cheers:

31

"Strawberry shortcake, blueberry pie!
V-I-C-T-O-R-Y!
Are we in it? No, we're not.
We're not in it, we're on *top*!"

She whirled cartwheels across the grass. Skill, pep, agility—those were what counted.

Whoops, she tumbled. Her dog, Heavenly Spot, romped into the cartwheeling. Dear dog, with the white spot on the end of his tail. Katie hadn't paid any attention to him for a week, so she gave Spot a good tussle, rolling in the grass with the beagle.

"Katie John," her mother's voice called from an upper window, "come up and get ready for supper. And bring the sheets from the drier."

Katie went in through the passageway under the side porch. The house was built on such a steep hill that back there the basement was the ground level. She was startled to hear the sound of a television set in the basement apartment along the passageway. Then she remembered her parents had mentioned they'd rented the apartment.

During the summer the house had been nearly free of renters, for the two rivermen were out on their towboats; Miss Howell, her fifth-grade teacher, had summered on her farm; and there had been only old Mr. Watkins in his top-floor room. And he slept during the day, because he was night watchman at the flour mill. Now the house was starting to fill up again.

Inside, Katie John stood for a moment before the heavy door to the fruit cellar. She hadn't smelled the fruit cellar for a long time. With anticipation she pulled the door open and sniffed the whiff of damp bricks and apples and oldness. The first sniff was always the best, for afterward the pent-up smell seemed to dissipate with the door open. To Katie, the smell was the essence of the house, hinting of the earth the house was planted in and ancient things stored in the cellar. The house had no attic for storage, the top-floor bedrooms being right under the flat roof. Once, in a wooden icebox in the fruit cellar, Katie John had found a stack of faded watercolors of flowers and river scenes, some ancestor's work. In all the clutter on the shelves were so many unknown treasures still to discover. . . .

Behind her the door opened from the basement apartment.

"Oh. I thought I heard somebody, and—" a voice trailed.

Katie saw a worn-looking woman wearing a drab housedress. The bright blare of the television set contrasted with the faded face and hump of shoulders.

The woman tried again. "I just thought maybe somebody was messing around, and—"

Katie realized she must have glared at the intruder and tried to smile. "I'm Katie John. I live here."

She couldn't even have her private time with the

fruit cellar without somebody butting in! Katie John thought she'd gotten over her resentment of sharing the beloved house with renters. After all, it had been her idea to rent out rooms so they could afford to live there. Dad still didn't earn enough money at his book writing to cover all their living costs and take care of a big old house.

"Cora Hitchens. I never lived in no basement before." The woman's voice was tired and whiny. "Down home at Joeville we had us— We're just staying here 'til we c'n git us a house. Hubby, he's got him a good job at the corn-products factory, and—"

"I hope you like it here," Katie said, closing the fruit-cellar door. "Excuse me, I've got to tend to the laundry." She made her escape through the furnace room into the laundry area.

Probably that woman had watched her practicing cheerleading, too!

Upstairs, arms full of sheets, she exclaimed to her mother, "Boy, that is one talkity lady downstairs! I just wish I could have a little privacy!"

"Oh, Katie, she's just lonely. Doesn't know anybody yet." Mrs. Tucker's eyes were always soft over wounded birds and stray people.

At the supper table in the back dining room, Katie's parents talked on, *diddle diddle*, about dull things, while she tried to count which boys might vote for her for cheerleader. Howard Bunch was on the team, and they'd always been good buddies.

Edwin didn't go out for the team. Jason—

"—got stuck on chapter four," Dad was saying. "Abby, must you always clean the third floor when I'm trying to write?"

"Well, I've got so much to do, next time you're stuck, *you* clean the third floor!" Mrs. Tucker's eyes didn't look soft at all.

Katie John studied her parents. They could never have had a magnificent romance like Heathcliff and Catherine in the book.

"Is it dull, being married?" she asked.

They looked at her, startled.

"Certainly not!" Dad said.

Katie tried to picture them courting. "Mother, why did you marry Dad?"

"My devilish glances overwhelmed her," Dad said, rolling spaghetti around his fork.

Mother snorted. "Actually, it was his strange sense of humor."

Katie John persisted. "But did you think he was— somebody wonderful?"

"Of course." Mother smiled. "I still do."

"Huh! The way you two were growling at each other?"

"Ah, but we were just working up a friendly little tiff," Dad said.

Katie didn't want jokes. She wanted answers. "Dad, what was it about Mother that you wanted to marry her for?" When he started to twinkle, she added, "Now tell me the truth!"

Her father continued to smile, but he answered seriously, "Well, Katie, your mother was the most kind-hearted girl I'd met . . . and sensible . . . and a great tennis partner. . . ."

"So it wasn't because she was pretty and exciting?"

Mother was looking down at her plate.

"That, too. Still is." Dad wiped his mouth with his napkin and leaned over and kissed Mother, who came out of the kiss smiling.

"Oh, you two are mucky!" Katie exclaimed, but she was pleased.

As she left the table, she wondered how Heathcliff and Catherine would have treated each other, if they'd just gotten married instead of having all that trouble.

In her room Katie John tried to study, but she kept thinking about Heathcliff and Catherine. How violently they had treated each other, as they grew up, hurting each other terribly—young Heathcliff outside in the cold dark, looking in the window at Catherine making friends with grand people, yearning for her. Real people didn't act like that. Katie didn't think she could stand it if Jason Schreiber pursued her with the savage intensity of Heathcliff. Good laws, no!

No, she told herself, Jason was simply a very interesting boy—Somebody Wonderful, maybe—and maybe someday she'd know more about what he was like. But really, all she wanted was to admire him from a distance.

Tuesday at school she found that was all that was possible. She saw him once in the halls, but she must have been invisible, because he didn't see her. In Homemaking class Jason was friendly, but he didn't pay any particular attention to her. Obviously, to him she was just another person, and that sharing time in the balloon hadn't meant to him what it had to her.

Sharing a balloon ride with Trish Hardwicke had not started any wonderful friendship with her, either. After Gym class, dressing in the locker room, Trish told some girls how absolutely thrilling the balloon ride was, especially the splash-and-dash on the river. Katie grinned at her gym shoes. Trish picked them up by mistake.

"Those are mine," Katie said, "see?" She indicated the *K.J.* she'd marked on the toes.

"Oh, yes." Trish dropped the shoes. "Oh, yes, you're the girl who was in the balloon."

"You went up too, Katie?" asked Priscilla Simmons. "Oh, sugar, you are so brave!"

"We saw Katie's funny old house," Trish said, tinkling a laugh. "Let's see, your folks run a boardinghouse for workmen, don't they?"

The way she said it, Katie John pictured a long table surrounded by paunchy men in undershirts,

37

belching. Priscilla, who lived on Partridge Avenue and ran with the country-club set, knew what Katie's house was like, but the other girls didn't.

"Not a boardinghouse," Katie John said. "Our renters don't eat with us. We rent out rooms in little apartments."

"They cook in their rooms?" Trish wrinkled her nose.

"Yes."

"Huh!" Trish laughed. "With all those cooking smells, you must never know what's for dinner, when you come home."

That sounded so pork-and-cabbagy. Katie John's face felt hot, and she couldn't think of a quick retort.

However, Priscilla said in her dear little voice, "At least she'll know there's *something.* At your house, Trish, what's for dinner is whatever your mother can boil up in a plastic bag."

The other girls laughed, and Katie John smiled at Priscilla. Priscilla was so nicety-sweet they'd never been close friends, but there must be some solid loyalty about going to the same grade school. And Priscilla was learning to salt all that sweetness.

Trish only shook her long hair carelessly. "That's only when Mum comes in late from golf. There *are* more important things than cooking."

On Wednesday Katie John admired Jason from a distance. She saw Trish catch up with him in the hallway and walk with him, and she loathed Trish Hardwicke from a distance.

Sue was walking down the hall with Katie, and she saw Katie looking at Jason and Trish.

"You think Jason is S.W., don't you?" Sue said. "Look, if you want to get something going, why don't I ask Bob to ask Jason if he likes you?"

"Good gosh, no! Don't start *anything!*"

"All right, Katie." Sue chuckled like a soothing mother hen.

But it seemed that Sue could not let go of the Somebody Wonderful business. At noon when Katie joined her in the lunchroom, Sue was sitting at a table with Lou Bee, a girl they both knew from sixth grade.

Sue was saying, "So, okay, Looby, who do you think is S.W.?"

The girl was one whom Katie John had wanted to know better, because she was a lively little person. Actually, her name was Louisa Beauty, but everyone called her Lou Bee or Looby. She was petite as a bird, with pert brown eyes, and while she'd probably never be a beauty, she certainly was getting pretty.

"S.W.? Hmm." Lou Bee cocked her head on one side, looking cute. "Well—Ramon."

"Ramon? Yes, he is," Sue encouraged her.

Hmph! Katie thought, chewing into her sandwich. She could have had a date with Ramon. If they only knew!

"And Eddie Jones," Lou Bee mused on.

"Uwk!" Katie choked on her lunch meat. "*Eddie!* Do you mean Edwin?"

"Yes, he's in Shop with me." Lou Bee nodded, her eyes sparkling. "I call him *Eddie* to see his face get pink."

"Katie John," Sue said hastily at the look on Katie's face, "tell who you think is S.W."

"Nobody!" Katie said loudly.

"Oh, come on, it's just for fun. You know, Ja—"

"Shut up, Sue!" She wanted to die. "Nobody! Nobody's wonderful!"

It was a dumb, awful conversation. Lou Beauty's bright eyes still watched her. She wished she'd never mentioned *smoky* or Jason. This was what she got for talking about boys with Sue.

Admiring from a distance meant not getting *involved.*

All afternoon Katie John concentrated on her classes. In Gym she did gymnastics. In History she learned history. In Art she did art.

After school she saw Ramon picking up a notebook by Lou Bee's locker. Looby was cocking her head at him. So scratch Ramon. Not that she wanted *anybody* trying to date her. It was all just—stupid. *Stew-pid.* Scott.

Jason went by in the hallway, and Katie refrained from saying hi to see if he'd say hi first. He didn't. He didn't seem to see her at all. Katie's first impulse was to stick a foot out and trip him. The second impulse was to cry. She whipped around toward her locker, because she felt crazy tears coming into her eyes.

"Say, Katie," Edwin's voice said behind her, "you want to come out and hunt geodes this afternoon?"

"Sure!"

Katie John whirled around and flashed Edwin such a grateful smile that Edwin muttered, "Good grief!"

However, all went comfortably. Edwin hiked Katie on his bike down to her house so she could get her bike and check in with her mother. Then they rode out to the old cemetery on the edge of town. And when Katie John pedaled in among the gravestones resting under the oak trees on the little hills and dales, she felt the same peace she always felt there. Yes, as always, a mourning dove was calling *hoo, hoo,* accentuating the peace. The place was like a private park to Katie, and coming out there was how she'd first gotten acquainted with Edwin.

Not talking, they cycled down the single-lane pavement that wound between rows of identical white stones, the National Cemetery that warranted a paid resident caretaker. Many a Civil War soldier was buried there, and Edwin's father had to be something of a historian, answering inquiries about dates on the grave markers or records of people's ancestors. Down by the creek, the town cemetery began: great granite stones, family tombs, a twelve-foot stone cross, the Black Angel—a bronze monstrosity that had turned black instead of patinaed green—then a section of stones incised with Hebrew letters, relics of the olden days when Barton's Bluff had contained a small but flourishing Jewish community.

"Here, wait." Edwin pulled open the iron door on a caretaker's shed and brought out two shovels. "For pecking around in the creek banks."

They went down into the dry rocky creek bed, where a few russet-brown oak leaves had already drifted. Katie could see where Edwin had dug up something.

"But I don't see any geodes." She'd rather expected to see some sparkling rocks.

"Not here," Edwin said. "The ones I found I carried up to the garage, so nobody would take them. Come on, I've searched this area pretty well. Let's head upstream a little."

Communication done, Edwin had nothing else to say, but that was all right. It was a good place for being quiet. In the small ravine, the creek banks got higher, almost up to their shoulders. Picking their way over rocks and sandy patches, they studied the creek bed for the rough round gray stones that could be geodes. Once Edwin dug a promising rock out of the sand, but it was flat on the bottom, the wrong shape.

They moved on. Katie liked hunting for things with Edwin. Last year they'd found a deserted house out in the hills and had explored it to learn

42

who had lived there. Still, the day at school kept nagging at her.

When they stopped to rest, their backs against the warm sand of the bank, she said, "How many geodes have you found, *Eddie*?"

Edwin's face turned pink. "Oh geez, don't call me that!"

"I know somebody who does," she teased. "Can't I call you Eddie, too?"

"Ah, cut it out, Katie John!" Looking mad, Edwin got up and poked his shovel at a rock. "You can call me Ed, if you want. That's what my uncle did, on the farm."

She got up, too, and stood close to him. "Then maybe you could call me Katherine?"

"Aw, what is this?" He moved away, his long nose flared as if he'd smelled something bad. "Let's keep looking for geodes, before the sun goes down."

Katie John sighed, following him. It was stupid to try any you-me stuff with him. Standing close to his stringy boy-body hadn't been anything exciting. Edwin wasn't S.W., even if Lou Bee wanted to think so.

But Jason was. Katie remembered his broad shoulders next to hers in the balloon basket and the shaggy blackness of his hair. She trailed behind Edwin so he couldn't see her face and get any hints of what she was thinking.

4

The Way to
a Man's Heart

As she bicycled home, Katie John scolded herself. *You ought to be ashamed, being so disloyal to your good friend, Edwin. This S.W. stuff is just nonsense!*

After supper she gave Heavenly Spot a good brushing and checked his floppy ears for ticks. Then she studied. Then she read a rousing good adventure story to clean her mind of romantic notions.

But the next day in Homemaking class Jason said, "Hey, Katie, can you show me what they mean about folding eggs into this batter?" And her body went all quivery again.

That night she resurrected her diary. In it she wrote, *There is a boy I like named Jason Schreiber. I don't think he likes me, but that's all right. I just admire him from a distance, as a friend.*

44

She felt soft and tentative as she wrote it. She sat back, read over the words and looked at them for a while. Then Katie John snorted. Who did she think she was kidding! She wanted Jason to like her.

If she were chosen as a cheerleader, he'd think she was somebody special.

Friday morning Katie John dressed as pleasingly as she could and brushed her brown hair out as long as it would go. On the way to school she was a little snappish with Sue and her chatter, because she was trying to go over the cheers in her mind to remember all of them.

"Mr. Carruthers' first name? I don't know, and I don't care."

*That's the way you spell it, that's—*no—*here's the way you yell it—*

"Sue, Bob's on the football team, isn't he? He'll vote for me, don't you think?"

"I don't know, and I don't care!"

What was Sue getting so huffy about?

"I should think you'd care whether I get elected cheerleader or not."

Sue fluffed her feathers—her hair. "I care just as much about what you care about as you care what—about—I care about!"

"Huh?" Katie giggled. "Tangle-tongue." She hugged Sue's shoulders.

And Sue got the giggles, too, so it was all right.

At the cheerleaders' tryouts after school, Katie John learned that the palms of her hands could prickle. She wondered if the boys on the team got this nervous before a game, knowing they had to get out in front of everybody and perform. The boys on the J.V. team sat in a roisterous horde up in the bleachers of the football field. Katie John sat down in front on the team's benches with the other girls trying out. All of them wore numbers on their chests, in case the boys didn't know their names. With the girls was Miss Bounce, their gym teacher.

It was wonderful the way people picked jobs to suit their names, Katie thought, trying to think about anything but cheerleading and prickling palms. Besides Miss Bounce, there was the priest at St. Francis Catholic Church named Father Patience. And, let's see—

"All right, girls, show 'em the old Locomotive," Miss Bounce said.

The eighth-grade girls performed first, and Katie John recognized that not only did they show a lot of pep, but every last one of the girls was pretty. She didn't know any of them, except a girl who was in her Homemaking class.

Then it was the seventh-grade girls' turn to get out there, first in a long line, then in fours. More seventh graders had turned out than eighth graders, as though the older girls only showed up if they really knew they had a chance. Katie John eyed her competitors: Trish Hardwicke—you might know!—Priscilla Simmons, Betsy Ann, Lou Bee, and a lot of other girls, some she'd seen in classes, some she'd never noticed before. There were fat girls, skinny girls, a girl whose red-gold hair curled around her head like a cap, a girl who had brown eyes and dimples.

"Victory, victory, victory!" With the lineup of girls Katie John jumped and threw her arms in the air.

She could see Jason's face in the throng of boys, but she couldn't tell whether he was looking at her.

Trish and three other girls stepped forward to do their stuff. "Strawberry shortcake, blueberry pie . . ." Watching from behind, Katie could see Trish was graceful enough. No pizazz, though.

When it was Katie's turn to step forward from the line, she swallowed hard, and her knees felt watery. How on earth could she *jump*?

The girl next to her said, "Hi, I'm Jackie," as cheerfully and easily as if butterflies only appeared on flowers, never in stomachs.

"Yeah. Katie John."

"Strawberry shortcake—" Katie put a smile on her face and pep into her movements. She kept an eye on Jackie to make sure she was coordinating with her. She made her legs and body lithe with every bit of skill and agility she possessed.

"Come on, Jackie!" a boy yelled from the bleachers.

Jackie laughed and shook her honey-brown hair, jumping. "We're on top!"

Katie leaped, too, and as the foursome broke up,

even though it wasn't part of the routine, she flared a cartwheel.

"Yay, Katie!" That was Howard Bunch's holler.

She grinned at the bleachers and got back in line.

When the tryouts were over, the girls sat anywhere on the grass, while the boys wrote names on the paper Miss Bounce passed out.

"Remember, boys, all of you vote for both seventh- and eighth-grade girls, four girls from each grade."

So Jason could vote for her, if he wanted. Katie John bit at a fingernail. Sue came over from the fence, where she'd been watching.

"It's a meat market," Sue muttered. "Now, don't you feel bad if you don't get elected, because you were just terrific anyway."

For a moment, Katie wondered why she should even care about boys, when she had a friend like Sue.

She could see Jason writing on his paper, but she hadn't seen him glance in her direction.

The ballots gathered in, Miss Bounce went into a huddle with two boys to tally the votes. The waiting seemed so long that Katie suddenly felt very hungry. She couldn't go over and visit with the boys the way some of the girls did.

"All right," Miss Bounce called over the growing hubbub, "here are your cheerleaders! As I call out the names, girls, please step forward in front of the bleachers. Beth Wowski." She began with the eighth graders.

One girl was beautiful with shining black braids. The next girl was beautiful with personality. So it went. The seventh graders: the brown-eyed girl with dimples, Trish Hardwicke—Katie groaned— Lou Bee and Jackie Peterson. The boys cheered and mock-groaned after each name was announced.

Katie John smiled and put her chin up. "Yay," she cheered and clapped with the other kids for the new cheerleaders.

Pep, skill and agility were all very well, but in Barton's Bluff, pretty and popular were what counted.

"So am I so ugly?" she demanded of her mirror that night.

Popular—what was that? You could only know so many people. Howard Bunch had assured her that he and Pete and Bob had voted for her, "and lots of other guys did," he'd added vaguely.

Ugly? Not so's you would shudder. But—pretty? No, there was nothing special about her looks. Thick brown hair that went spiky at her forehead, because she had a bad habit of shoving her fingers up through her hair. Gray-green eyes, just okay eyes. Her face used to be scrawny, but it was filling out— if she didn't cut down on the cookies, her face might become positively fat! Her body was still slim enough, though.

But I don't look like anybody romantic, Katie John thought mournfully.

How could she get Jason to like her? Maybe it was impossible.

Still, she could study how to be nice to him, without acting all cute and silly.

Monday morning Katie John was out in the vegetable garden, where a red cardinal kept her company as it pecked around in the tangle of grapevines on the alley fence. The early-morning sweetness of the air made Katie feel so good she sang, "A little lettuce here, some red tomatoes there," as she gathered them for the salad. That day she was one of several who were to prepare a complete meal for the Homemaking class. Katie John had chosen to make the salad, because it sounded the easiest and because the garden at home was bursting with vegetables. She took three heads of lettuce, to make sure she had enough. And plenty of green onions— she shook the good black dirt off as she pulled them, so the dirt could go back to growing more things. And what else? There were still some peas, and little crisp peas were nice in a salad.

Katie wanted her salad to be the best ever, for she had heard Jason say the thing he liked best about the cooking class was eating. She'd take some of Mother's homemade oil-and-vinegar dressing and, in case Jason preferred something else, she would stop at the corner grocery and buy some blue-cheese dressing.

Katie and Sue carried their sacks of supplies to school. Sue was doing the dessert, so in her sack she had the makings for brownies: box mixes, eggs and a can of prepared chocolate frosting.

"Anybody can cook from a box or a can," Katie teased.

"Huh! I can make fudge from scratch, and you know it!"

"Anyway, it's going to be a super meal, yum."

The main dish was to be spaghetti. Priscilla, who was also in the class, and another girl were to make the sauce, and Jason had been appointed to cook the spaghetti.

Shifting her sack of vegetables to her other arm, Katie John looked back to see if Jason was coming along. It was strange that she had almost never seen him walking to and from school since that first day. Of course, he would have football practice after school, but in the mornings either he went earlier than she and Sue did, or he must go a different route.

"I'll tell you something," Sue was saying, "although I don't suppose you really care." Now her voice was teasing.

"What?"

"After the tryouts last night, Bob told me Jason said he voted for you."

"Huh!"

"Now you owe me one."

"Okay." Belatedly, Katie realized the significance of the conversation. "Oh, Sue, you didn't tell Bob I like Jason, did you?"

She shrugged, smiling.

"Sue Halsey! Please, please, don't talk about it to anybody."

Sue kept on grinning. "So who's talking? I only reported what Bob said."

The cooking class was chaos. Katie John thought surely it must be easier for one person to get a dinner ready in an hour than seven people, with all the others milling around. Mrs. Bartlett darted from the sauce people—"Your burger's burning!"—to the French-bread person, who sliced his finger along with the bread—"Good cooks never bleed on the bread!" Tearing up lettuce and slicing tomatoes, Katie worried she'd never have her huge salad ready in time. She admired the calm way Sue mixed up her brownie batter and popped the pans into an oven, even remembering to set the timer. Sue came over to help Katie chop green onions into the fourth big bowl of salad.

"Katie John," Jason called from their team's stove, "could you take a look at this?"

Gladly!

He was poking at two big boiling pots. "It ought to be done, but it doesn't look right."

Katie peered through the steam. In each pot was a great glob of spaghetti sticking together.

"I threw it in like she said, when the water boiled," he said helplessly.

Katie John could hardly stand the way his eyes appealed to her. "I guess you have to keep stirring it while it cooks," she said. "I didn't know that before, either. Here, maybe I can chop it apart some."

With a long spoon she poked at a spaghetti lump until she got a lot of the strands uncongealed.

"Try it like that on the other lump." She handed the spoon to Jason.

"Thanks, Katie!" He squeezed her shoulders.

"Oh!"

Did it mean anything? It was definitely a hug.

Deliberately Katie said, "You and I together wouldn't make one good cook!"

She wanted to see if he'd look at her in that personal way again.

But Jason was already poking at the other spaghetti pot, and he only said, "Um," not turning back to her.

Had it been too bold a thing to say—the part about "you and I together"? Anyway, Jason had hugged her, so—

But when it was time to eat the meal, a terrible thing happened. Jason said no thanks, he never ate salad. He wasn't even going to touch the food she had prepared! And there she was, trying to swallow his lumpy spaghetti.

"But I just picked it all fresh this morning from our garden." Katie John tried to keep the wail out of her voice.

"Oh, I'm sure it's very good," Jason said. "I just don't like salad."

Nor did the other boys in the class. To a man, they

all said no, they weren't too hungry, so they'd just eat the spaghetti and bread.

Then Priscilla squealed, "Katie John! Did you know there's a *worm* in this salad? A fat green worm!"

And Katie snapped, "Yes, Priscilla, I put it there just for you!"

It didn't help that Sue whispered, "You're supposed to wash the lettuce. That's how you sort out the worms."

Giggle giggle. Of course, Sue could giggle! Katie saw that the not-too-hungry boys could finish off Sue's brownies to the last crumb. The way to a man's heart might be through his stomach, but not with salad.

At the end of the lunch hour, two of the big bowls of greenstuffs remained untouched.

"What am I going to do with all this salad?" Katie John exclaimed to Mrs. Bartlett.

The salad had been good, too, except that the peas were really too big and old for eating raw.

"Oh, I was going to ask you," Mrs. Bartlett said. "May I have it? I'm having a dinner party tonight, and I'd be—"

"Sure!" She helped the teacher put the salad into plastic bags.

The next blow of the day came in Gym class, although Miss Bounce probably thought she was being nice. In front of everybody she asked Katie John to head up a kazoo band.

"For fun at the games." Miss Bounce was brisk. "You showed such pep at the tryouts, Katie, I just know you'll do a good job."

She hummed some wheezy toots on the kazoo, and all the girls laughed.

Handing the kazoo to Katie John, Miss Bounce said, "You'll do it, won't you? I have four more kazoos, so if you'll get four girls—"

Katie stood there, horrified. How could you say no to a teacher? But, a kazoo band! Instead of being a glamorous cheerleader, she was supposed to be the Class Clown!

The smile on Trish Hardwicke's face was pure glee.

"I don't know," Katie stalled. "What kind of—"

"Jazz it up, the funnier the better. Now then, girls." Miss Bounce went on with the day's activities, leaving Katie with the kazoo in her limp hand.

Naturally, none of the girls would agree to be in a kazoo band.

"I don't think I'm funny enough," Priscilla said, her mouth tight. She hadn't forgiven Katie's crack about the worm.

"Sue?"

"I'm sorry. You know I'd do almost anything for you. But you see it, don't you? We'd just be making fools of ourselves to get out there in a kazoo band."

At the end of class Katie John tried to give the wheezy whistle back to the teacher. "I can't be a one-man kazoo band."

But Miss Bounce insisted, "No, no, you keep it. I'll find some girls in the next class, and you'll be the leader!"

After school Sue had to go to her piano lesson, so Katie John walked home alone. She didn't look at anything but the pavement of the sidewalk. Which was broken in a lot of places. What was the point of trying to attract a boy, when nothing went right? That hug of Jason's hadn't meant anything. Katie shoved her hands into her jacket pockets and felt the kazoo.

Stupid thing! She ought to throw it as far as she could! A clown! That's all anybody thought she was good for. Whereas probably she couldn't even play the stupid thing.

She breathed into the hole on one end and achieved a wheeze like the rattly sound of blowing on a comb wrapped in thin paper. Actually, it wheezed better than the comb effect she remembered getting when she was little. Sadly Katie hummed into the kazoo the strains of "Old Folks at Home." "How my heart grows weary, far from the old folks at home," the kazoo sighed.

She rounded a corner and came upon some little kids playing on the sidewalk.

"What is that thing?" asked a boy in a small wagon.

"A kazoo." Katie John blew a fluttery toot at him.

"Play it! Play!" demanded the little-bit-bigger girl who was pulling the wagon.

Katie wheezed, "Way down upon the—" But that was too sad, so she switched to "The Stars and Stripes For Ever." "Whee whee wheezle whee wheezle whee," she blew, "wheezle whee wheezle whee wheezle wheeee wheeee. . . ." She walked backward up the sidewalk as she played, and the little girl followed her, hauling the wagonload of boy. At the blare of the kazoo, another little boy ran out from between two houses. At the next house, two more children ran down from a front porch and joined the sidewalk parade. "Wheezle whee whee wheeee!" Katie laughed. She felt like the Pied Piper. She turned around to march ahead of the kids, giving her all to the kazoo finish, "Whee whee whee wheetly-wheet!"

"Ha ha ha!" somebody burst out laughing in the street behind. It was Edwin on his bicycle.

Katie John looked at him, grinning.

"Katie John, you are the—" Edwin shook his head, still laughing. "You are the most— I don't know!"

Whatever he meant to say, it was something good about her. She felt warm inside. There she'd been, just trundling along, being her stupid self, not trying to be attractive, and somebody thought she was likable.

"Hey, Edwin—Ed—what are you doing down this way?"

The little boy in the wagon was begging, "Let me try, let me try it," so she handed him the kazoo.

"Oh." Edwin shrugged, smiling. "An errand—uh, for Dad."

Whatever the errand was, he didn't seem in any hurry to do it. Katie John got the kazoo back from the children and wheezed good-bye to them, and Edwin walked his bike all the way home with her.

So the day wasn't totally lost, after all.

5

The Old Maid's Life

Playing the kazoo for little kids and making Edwin laugh out loud was one thing. Playing the kazoo at the football game Friday afternoon and making the whole school laugh was a different matter. Katie John wondered if maybe she and the girls could tootle once unobtrusively, and that would be the end of it. But she realized there was no way to slink through a kazoo-band performance. Either they did it with pep and foolishness, or they shouldn't do it at all.

Against Katie's hopes, Miss Bounce turned up four other girls willing to make fools of themselves—or unwilling to say no to the teacher.

After school Katie and the girls, whom she hadn't met before, practiced on their kazoos. And the sound of five of them trying to wheeze together on "The Stars and Stripes For Ever" was so funny they couldn't help laughing.

"So okay, we're the Five Kazoo Clowns," Katie John said recklessly, "and we'll just do it up *bang*, the best we can!"

And they did Friday at the J.V. game, and everybody laughed and clapped, and whether anybody scorned her as a fool, Katie didn't know. She'd hoped somehow Jason would be too busy with the game to notice the kazoo band, but she saw him watching and grinning with the other guys.

During the week he'd been nice enough to her in class, but since the hug nothing personal had happened between them. On the other hand, while watching him in class and glimpsing him in the halls and lunchroom, she hadn't noticed anything personal between him and any other girl—not even Trish Hardwicke, who looked beautiful as a model in her new cheerleader's outfit.

So why are you so depressed? Katie demanded of herself Friday night.

In her rather isolated room in the back wing of the second floor, she'd sat at Great-Aunt Emily's little old desk with her chin in her hands, thinking and feeling miserable for hours, it seemed.

The trouble was, she wasn't a romantic-type girl, and she probably never would be! With shame she remembered how she'd gotten carried away with playing the kazoo at the game, trotting up and

60

down, wagging her head, as she led the girls. She'd actually enjoyed being funny with the kazoo—and she was stupid!

Catherine Earnshaw, in *Wuthering Heights*, was as romantic as a gypsy. She was darkly beautiful and willful and imperious, and she never, never would have played a kazoo. If she had, Heathcliff would have looked at her in amazement and disgust.

You are a dumb stupid clown, Katie thought, being just as mean and punishing to herself as she could, *and no boy will ever call you his "heart's darling"!*

Tears spurted out, and she just sat there and cried, absentmindedly wiping up the tears that spotted the old walnut wood of the desk.

"What on earth?" Her mother came into the room.

"No boy will ever like me!" Katie John wailed.

Then she hid her face and hated herself more, because the last person she meant to tell anything about it was her mother. Probably her mother had *always* been pretty.

"Why, Edwin likes you."

"Oh, *Edwin*! That's not what I mean!" She put her head down on the desk and sobbed.

Mrs. Tucker smoothed her hand over Katie's rough hair. "Oh, honey, don't cry so. Boys your age just aren't interested in girls yet."

"Yes, they are!" Katie wailed.

"Then choose one of them."

She'd already blown her chances with Ramon. He was always hanging around Lou Bee. And she didn't care, anyway.

"I can't." She sobbed. "Not the one I like."

"Oh." Mrs. Tucker's voice was soft. "Honey, I know."

Katie John kept on crying, and finally her mother said, "Why I came up here, Katie—Katie? Listen. Tomorrow will you go with me to the Collingwood sisters' house and help clean it? They've been sick, and I don't think they can afford a cleaning lady, even if they could find one."

Katie's head came up. "Spend the day with four old-maid sisters? That's what you think I'm good for? Oh well," she said dismally, "I might as well take lessons to be an old maid."

Mrs. Tucker retreated.

Barton's Bluff had a goodly population of old ladies. Some were old and crotchety, like Miss Crackenberry, who lived next door beyond the vegetable gardens. Some were old and socially prominent. Some were kindly available as baby-sitters. Some could barely totter down the streets on their genteel, meager errands.

The Collingwood sisters didn't seem to fit any of those categories. There were four of them, although Katie John had seen only the three who came regularly to church: Mamie, Myrtle and Maude. There was a fourth sister, Esther, who never went out, and Katie wondered for the first time why she was so mysteriously tucked away. They all lived together in a grand old brick house with corners tiered in white marble. The story in Barton's Bluff was that the marble pieces were tombstone rejects from the Civil War soldiers' cemetery; old Mr. Collingwood, grandfather of the four sisters, had bought up the marble at a good price when he'd built the house back in the 1880's.

Saturday morning Katie John stood on the front steps of the Collingwood house with her mother. Although Katie had delivered things to the door, such as vegetables from the garden, she had never been farther into the house than the entrance room.

So okay, she thought, as she listened to the door chimes sound distantly inside, if she was a dumb clown and never possibly desirable like Catherine Earnshaw, then she'd just see what the old maid's life was like. After all, Great-Aunt Emily had chosen the single life and had seemed to be quite content with it. Katie remembered how she'd ferreted out clues to the young Emily's romance with a man she'd finally refused. I can *choose* not to marry, Katie John thought, feeling brave.

Inside there was, as always, the sound of yipping and the scrabbling of toenails on the marble tiled floor. Fritz was the doorman. He was a black-and-white Boston terrier with bulging eyes and an insistent manner, and those toenails could scratch.

"No, Fritz, no, no," said Myrtle, one of the middle sisters, who opened the door.

Nevertheless, the terrier jumped all over Katie's legs and scraped them. The entrance room fairly thronged and echoed with the yapping dog and a bustle of three old ladies, who chattered and coughed.

"Oh, Mrs. Tucker, so good of you—uff cuff."

"And you brought your little girl—oh dear!"

"Naughty, naughty, Fritzie!"

The two older sisters wore heavy sweaters buttoned across their chests, and Maude was hunched in a long shawl. It was no wonder the Collingwood sisters had colds. Although it was fairly warm outside, they had all the windows closed, and it was cool inside the house, as if last winter's chill was still trapped there. There was a dry, medicinal smell to the place.

The commotion of them progressed into a long drawing room, where Katie John got more impressions of marble: a carved white marble fireplace with a great mirror over it, and beside it a marble statue of an angel. The room was elegant with velvet settees and marble-topped tables and a harp— a harp!—standing in a corner. But the room was trashed with torn-up newspapers, which Fritz ran to chew on and worry. There was a heavy film of dust over the furniture and a bewildering variety of antique ornaments sitting around. And when Katie edged over to inspect the golden harp, she saw a pile of Fritz's droppings behind it.

She smothered a giggle and politely, through the clatter of talk, asked Mamie, "Do you play the harp?"

"Oh, no. Maude is our musician!"

Maude nodded, clutching her shawl, and said to Mrs. Tucker, "But I haven't been able to practice lately, I've been so—" She broke off, coughing.

Katie John studied the three old-maid sisters. Mamie, the oldest, was large and gray and comfortable-looking as a fat tabby cat. She was, however, bossy.

"Myrtle, get out the vacuum cleaner for Mrs. Tucker. Maude, do something for that poor little dog."

Little Myrtle, with her knobby, busy face, was as vigorous and chattery as a squirrel.

"Oh, Mrs. Tucker, I'm ashamed to have you see our house like this. I like to keep it clean, but I've felt so worthless, and Monday the ladies of St. Cecilia's Guild are coming, and—"

Maude, a rather pretty, plumpish woman, didn't remind Katie of any animal—unless it was Fritz himself, humored and yappity.

"I've been the sickest," she said, "and I have to be careful, you know, because I have a weak chest, and—"

"Yes, Maude's been the sickest," Myrtle said, "and we can't do without Maude, because she's our shopper. She goes out and buys all our supplies. Of

65

course, we can't do without you, either, Mamie, to cook our meals."

"And we can't do without you, Myrtle," Mamie said heavily, "because we can't have Mrs. Tucker coming to clean more than once."

"Well, I must say, I can't help it if—" Myrtle protested, and the three of them began to fuss at each other.

Mrs. Tucker broke that up by saying, "I'll just find the vacuum," and moving toward the hallway. Myrtle hurried after her.

"And I'll get started on the dusting," Katie said, whipping out the dustcloth she'd brought.

She was used to dusting her way through a thicket of antique knickknacks left behind at her own house by Great-Aunt Emily. With a professional eye, she reached for a tinkling glass tree that stood on one end of the marble mantelpiece.

"Oh, no, no!" cried Myrtle, coming back into the drawing room with Mrs. Tucker and an ancient upright vacuum cleaner. "The little girl might B-R-E-A-K something," she spelled out to Katie's mother.

It had to be funny. The only thing to do was laugh. Katie John grinned at her mother, who pressed her lips together to keep her mouth in control as she plugged in the vacuum. Fritz began to bark at the humming machine.

"Maybe I could clean up after the dog."

Katie scuttled on the floor after pieces of torn newspaper, while the terrier tried to jump on her.

66

She shook him off and with a wad of paper headed for the pile behind the harp.

Myrtle, following her, saw the pile and exclaimed, "Oh, poor little Fritzie! None of us have felt well enough to take him out regularly." She trotted away to get a sack for the trash.

Over the noise of the talking and barking and vacuum buzzing Mrs. Tucker called, "Maybe Katie could take Fritz out now."

"Oh, I don't know if Fritz would—walk—for her," Maude worried.

"Sure he will," Katie John assured her. "I've got a dog of my own."

Heavenly Spot was a good wholesome *dog*, who sometimes came in with a little mud on his feet, not a snippy little house toy! Katie whisked Fritz's harness onto him, even though he nipped at her fingers.

"Whee-sh!" She breathed a sigh of relief when she got outside the cold noisy house with the dog. Holding the leash, she led him toward the curb.

Immediately there was a tapping sound on a front window, and the window went up. "Don't take him in the *street*!" Myrtle called.

So Katie pulled Fritz, who wanted to go in the street, around to the lawn at the side of the house. Just as the terrier was starting to hump, there was a tapping on a side window, which went up.

The shawled head of Maude called out, "Don't let him go on the *grass*!"

Katie hauled the nasty little beast around to the back of the house, where Mamie threw up a kitchen window to call, "Not in the laundry yard! Take him to the alley."

Finally Katie got the dog out of sight behind a brick carriage barn. Poor little Fritzie, to live with such a bunch of women! If those sisters were any example, growing up to be an old maid could be dreadful. She'd better plan to have some kind of a career and keep her mind busy.

Going back, Katie let Fritz sniff around while she looked up at the high brick house. Even at the rear, where no one could admire them, white marble blocks were set into the brickwork at the corners all the way to the top. As Katie looked, there was a movement at an upper window. A face was watching her. Then the face was gone, the window blank.

The fourth sister! It must be. She'd forgotten about the other woman. In all the chatter, she realized, the Collingwood sisters had not once mentioned their sister, Esther.

Suddenly Katie John was reminded of *Jane Eyre*. Somewhere in the book, hadn't Jane looked up at the mansion and seen a face at a window? It had been that of a madwoman kept locked away. Was Esther insane, and so never to be talked of? Did she rage in her lonely room the way the madwoman did?

Katie wondered how she could get upstairs to

learn the secret of the house. Did she have the nerve?

There was nothing sinister about the big old-fashioned kitchen when Katie John led the scampering dog in that way. Mamie was putting loaves of homemade bread into the oven, and she handed Katie a little raspberry tart from a plate on the table.

"Here, eat this for energy."

While she ate it, Myrtle and Maude came out to the kitchen to greet Fritz after his arduous journey outside with a stranger, and unhitch him from his harness. The three sisters consulted and fussed and finally decided that probably Katie could clean the downstairs bathroom without harming it. However, Myrtle stood over her to supervise. The way the old ladies kept stirring around over the cleaning session, Katie thought, they were using so much energy they might as well have done the cleaning themselves.

Mamie came to the bathroom door. "She could clean Esther's room."

"Oh yes," Myrtle said at once. "She couldn't hurt anything there!"

"No!" Mamie snorted.

That easily she'd get to see Esther!

The women loaded Katie up with cleaning supplies: dustpan and broom, scrub bucket and mop. What kind of a room, what kind of a mess, was it?

As directed, Katie John started up the very dark well of a back staircase. As she mounted in the darkness, the noise of chatter and yipping faded away. There was not a sound from above. In the upper hallway she turned left through dead air. The house didn't breathe, as her old house seemed to.

They wouldn't send a little girl up to clean a madwoman's room, would they?

The door to the room was closed. Katie set down the mop and broom and tapped gingerly on the paneling of the door. There was a sudden fluttering sound from within. She waited and knocked again.

"Yes?" came the faint whisper of a voice.

Moving the door open a little, Katie John peered inside, and her eyes were dazzled with light. The September sun poured through three uncurtained windows of the large room. Blinking, Katie John made out a wheelchair and in it, a two-headed woman. One head flew off.

No! Katie gasped, her knees trembling. It wasn't a head; it was a bird. As her eyes adjusted to the brightness, she realized the large light-colored bird had been sitting on the woman's shoulder next to her white head. It flew in swoops around the room, its wings making a rattling sound.

"Close the door," the woman said. "Don't let Gulliver out."

Katie John closed herself into the room. The downstairs sisters had been old, but the upstairs sister was *really* old. She was so small she must have shrunk, for the wheelchair looked too big for her. Her face was a soft crumple of wrinkles, and pink

70

scalp showed through wisps of her shining white hair. Bright little nut eyes looked through gold-rimmed spectacles at Katie.

"I'm Katie John Tucker," she whispered. "May I clean your room?"

She couldn't stop staring, not only at the tiny woman, but at the cages. On a tall pole hung a gilt cage, into which the bird fluttered. On the floor filling one corner of the room stood an enormous cage made of gilded scrolls of metal. It was big enough to hold a person.

"Yes, it needs it," the old lady replied. She added, as Katie stood staring, "Well?" And then, gently, "Welcome, my dear."

Surely a person with a voice that gentle wouldn't go to raging and have to be locked in a cage.

"Thank you," Katie whispered.

She retrieved the mop and broom, which she'd shut out in the hall. The room certainly did need it. Besides the unmade bed and the dust on the furniture—was that antique thing a sewing machine?—Gulliver's litter was all over the floor: bird droppings, birdseed and scraps of paper the bird was ripping with its beak from the bottom of its dirty cage. Downstairs the floor Fritz had littered was covered with a faded but beautiful carpet. Here the floor was covered with linoleum.

As Katie went to work sweeping the floor, the woman said not a word but picked up some sewing work from her lap.

Managing to get her voice to a normal pitch, Katie John asked, "Have you had a bad cold, too, Miss Collingwood?"

"No"—Esther didn't look up from her sewing—"they don't come up here enough to give me a cold." She made a funny little sound that Katie realized was a laugh.

The bird flew to its mistress' shoulder and made the same soft chuckling sound.

"What a beautiful bird!" Katie exclaimed.

Its feathers, looking soft as velvet, were pale brown with a faint pink tinge, and circling the back of its neck was a black ring. Sweeping the broom closer, Katie saw the bird had red feet and a red eye that peeped at her.

"I'd a lot rather clean up your litter than Fritzie's," she told the bird, who watched her silently.

"Hmph!" The little lady smiled.

"Ma'am, what kind of a bird is it?"

The nut eyes peeped at her, too. "He's some kind of dove. He flew in my window one day and has never left, my Gulliver."

The bird *clutter*ed softly.

"I know why you call him that!" Katie John exclaimed. "*Gulliver* is the very sound he makes."

"Aha!" Esther looked at Katie with pleasure. "You are the first to guess!"

"How do you know he's a he?" Katie asked and then thought she shouldn't have asked that of an old maid.

"Well, he hasn't laid an egg!"

Miss Esther was a friendly person, Katie decided, even though she didn't chatter like the downstairs sisters. While she cleaned out the birdcage, she set out to learn as much as she could venture to ask.

"Don't you ever go downstairs?"

"Oh yes. After all, it's half mine. That's the trouble."

Katie looked at the old lady doubtfully. Was she senile?

"When Papa died, he left the house half to me and half to the other girls. Daughters by his second marriage, you know."

"Oh!"

No wonder there was the obvious division of three against one, rather like between Cinderella and her stepsisters. Katie thought it was as if she had come up through a dark tower into a bright solarium with an ancient princess in it. She liked the solitary old woman and her beautiful *clutter*ing bird.

Katie made the bed, and then in a closetlike bathroom she ran water into the scrub bucket and began to mop the floor, careful not to swash water onto the wheelchair. Miss Esther must have had polio or some wasting disease, for beneath her long skirt her legs were thin as sticks. Probably she'd had no choice but to be an old maid.

In a small voice Katie said, "Miss Collingwood, what can I do for you?"

Not hearing, crickling that birdlike chuckle, the old lady mused over her sewing, "Papa was very bad. Gave me half to punish them. But they would torment him so about his business." She stopped, and the dove preened a wisp of her hair.

"Hm?" Katie prompted her.

"Wholesale liquor dealer, he was." She bit off a thread. "They said they'd never live down the shame of it, couldn't go out socially, could never marry. Silly fools."

Katie thought about that while she mopped the floor under the birdcage. Yes, a person would be a fool to give up caring about boys for silly reasons. Out of the next silence, the old lady spoke to her.

"Tucker. You must be Emily Clark's niece."

"Great-niece," Katie said, surprised at the lapse. "Oh, did you know my Great-Aunt Emily?"

"She was my dear friend." The woman looked away from Katie out the window. "Such an active life Emily led. I always thought I'd go first." She sighed and picked up her sewing. She murmured, "Earn my keep doing the mending."

Two old-maid friends once two young girls, Emily and Esther . . . "Did you know her when she was young?" Katie John asked eagerly. "Did she ever talk about—well—boys?"

The old eyes peered across the room at her as if she were at the end of a long tunnel. "Boys?" Miss Esther sewed a bit. "Emily turned down—what was his name?—when he came home from the war, fat and pompous, and after that no one took her fancy."

"Didn't she mind? I mean—"

"Yes, I think she did. She looked for a while." The crumpled face smiled. "But she made a good life, anyway."

And so, perhaps, had this aged Cinderella whose prince had never come. Miss Esther had her lifelong friend; she had her beautiful bird; and her mind seemed pithy enough despite a few old-age lapses.

"Do you think about boys?" The question darted.

Katie John mopped at a corner; but she saw the woman and the dove watching her.

"Sometimes."

"That's right." Esther nodded. "Male and female created He them."

Katie thought she must be quoting from the Bible about Adam and Eve.

"Does anyone come to see you now?" she asked, putting the cleaning supplies by the door.

"Oh, yes. Every week Reverend Speedwell comes and tells me how his sermon went. Then he takes off his collar, and we plot new ways to snare Christians." She chuckled merrily. "Fish for them, I guess I should say."

"Might I come to see you, too?" Maybe she didn't want lessons in the old-maid life, after all, but there was an enchantment about the old lady and her bird.

Esther cocked her head, looking at Katie. "Yes, perhaps. Not too soon—but don't wait too long."

Below them a bell clanged, startling Katie John. The dove fluttered up to its cage, and the lady put away her sewing.

"Time for homemade soup and bread," she said.

"Shall I—" Katie moved toward the chair. How could she get it down the dark stairs?

But Esther was already wheeling herself into the large cage. She pulled the gate shut and tugged on a knob. The cage began to sink. Of course. It was an elevator.

"Mayda wiggle woggle wee!" called the little woman, as if chanting a spell, as her head sank out of sight.

"What!"

"And may the world go well with thee," the words floated back.

Katie John laughed, and the dove chuckled.

6

Looking for Catherine

Katie John felt as if she had been the enthralled participant in a dream sequence during the interlude at the Collingwood sisters' house. Like one still gripped by the intense reality of a dream, at school she regarded Jason from a certain distance. He was just a boy; he wasn't so much. And yet, she noticed, there was that way he had of tossing his dark hair off his forehead.

Then people began talking about the Dance. The Homecoming Dance for both the Junior Varsity and the ninth-grade football teams was to happen a week from Saturday night.

In the lunchroom, Sue said, "It was at the Junior High dances that Janet started dating. I tell you, Katie John, it's hard to have a big sister who has *always* been popular!"

"Yes, but you always know what's coming, from watching Janet," Katie John said. "Do people go in couples to this dance, or can anybody go?"

"Oh, anybody. You're going, aren't you? The good part is to see which boys ask a person to dance."

"And if they don't?" Katie kept salting her bowl of stew. "What if nobody asks?"

"Well— Oh, Katie, they will."

Edwin slid onto the bench across the table from the girls.

Katie John took a bite of stew. "Yuck!"

"Thanks a lot," Edwin said.

"Oh, it's the stew. I salted it too much. Edwin, you're going to the dance, aren't you?"

"Nope." He set to work eating his stew methodically, potatoes first, then the meat, then the carrots and the other stuff.

"But you've got to go!" Katie John exclaimed. "Who will I dance with, if you don't go?"

It occurred to her that maybe Edwin didn't know how to dance. In sixth grade, the steps they'd learned in Gym classes hadn't progressed past square dancing.

"You don't have to go, either." Edwin glanced at her. "You know, you don't have to do all that stuff." He worked past the carrots.

Yes, I do! she thought. Part of her wanted to do all that stuff. She poked at her salty stew.

78

Sue tried to help. She said, "Bob is coming down to my house after school, and we're going to practice dancing. You want to come, too, Edwin?"

"Nope. Thanks." After a forkful of cole slaw, he got on with his dessert.

Maybe it was just as well Edwin wouldn't be at the dance. It was a test, Katie John recognized. If Jason asked her to dance, it might mean something. If he danced with other girls and not with her—well, that would mean something, too.

At a dance, a girl just had to be attractive.

That night Katie went to bed with a plate of chocolate chip cookies and *Wuthering Heights.* Propped up in her tidy little spool bed that had been Great-Aunt Emily's, she leafed through the book to find descriptions of Catherine Earnshaw when she was a girl. What was it about her that made Heathcliff so crazy about her?

Reaching for a cookie, Katie read what the old housekeeper told of Cathy: "Her spirits were always at high-water mark . . . singing, laughing and plaguing everybody who would not do the same. A wild, wicked slip she was—but she had the bonniest eye, the sweetest smile and the lightest foot in the parish."

Hmph. Catherine had been twelve then. Katie John munched down another cookie, while she found the page where Heathcliff talked to the housekeeper about Cathy: "beautiful hair . . . enchanting face . . . so immeasurably superior to everybody on earth." He admired her bravery, too. Cathy laughed with him when they were punished, and she "scorned to yell" when a bulldog seized her ankle.

Katie munched and read on, but finally she tossed the book away. Be like Catherine? Heaven forbid! The older Cathy got, the more willful and vicious she acted. Actually, Heathcliff was pretty much of a monster, too.

So what was it that fascinated her about them? Katie John mused as she ate the last cookie from the plate.

It was the way they cared about each other. That was it: their terrible allegiance to each other.

The next day on the way to school Katie told Sue, "I'm going to have my ears pierced."

"Katie *John*! You?"

Last spring when Sue had had her ears pierced, Katie had declared, "That's a dumb thing to do!" However, she'd noticed what a feminine gesture it was when Sue touched the little gold button in her ear.

"Yes, me! Why not?"

"Oh, sure, you'll love it! It makes a person feel so elegant." Lifting her chin, Sue swung the pearl-drop earrings she wore that day.

"Yeah!"

It was Katie's father who had to be persuaded. He objected, "Aren't you living pretty dangerously? First a balloon flight, and now pierced ears?" To his wife he added, "I'm not ready for the sight of Katie John hanging upside down on her trapeze with earrings dangling down."

"Oh, Dad! You make it sound so—"

"Now, Hugh, it'll be all right," Mother comforted him. "She's just—"

Katie fled, so she wouldn't hear herself talked about. By the next day her father had grudgingly agreed.

"But she'll have to pay for it herself."

The ear piercing cost ten dollars at the shopping-mall jewelry store, where a nurse was on duty on Saturday mornings. And then a person had only the first little gold buttons in her ears. Katie John was determined to buy also the prettiest, most feminine, dangliest earrings she could find. She was going to wear them to the Dance.

However, her funds had been depleted by the cost of the balloon flight. She'd accumulated only ten dollars since then. Instead of an allowance, she received five dollars a week for helping to clean the house. Though in a way she knew she shouldn't receive money for that. Two years ago she'd offered to help her mother with all the work of renting out rooms, if only the Tuckers could stay on in the house. It had been some sacrifice, because Katie John hated housework. And there was plenty of it.

Of course, her fifth-grade teacher and the lady in the basement took care of their apartments, but every Saturday Mrs. Tucker and Katie John cleaned and did the laundry for Mr. Watkins' and the river-men's rooms and bathrooms. All the hallways and staircases were a job in themselves. Plus, there was the variety of rooms that the Tuckers themselves used. Katie always cleaned Dad's writing room, because he said, "Abby's too tidy. Katie knows how to whisk over the surface and not bother my stacks of papers and books." Last Saturday, after they'd cleaned the Collingwood house, Katie John and her mother had gone home and worked until bedtime getting the Tucker housework done.

Friday after school Katie changed all the beds, and Saturday morning she hastened through her share of the work. She collected five dollars for that, then begged from her mother an advance on the following week's pay.

"So I'll have enough. While I'm there, I might as well pick out some real earrings besides the trainer posts, or whatever they call 'em."

"Shall I help you pick them out? Your first earrings," Mrs. Tucker said wistfully. "I'd kind of like to be along."

"Oh." Oh dear. "Well, actually, Mother, I think I ought to—"

"Yes, you're a big girl now. All right, run along." Her mother smiled as she gave Katie's bottom a light spank.

As Katie John hurried up the hallway toward the front door, Dad came out of the parlor. The morning was nearly gone. If the nurse left the jewelry store— Katie looked at her father impatiently.

"It isn't every day a girl gets her ears pierced. Treat yourself to lunch and a movie," he said, handing her a five-dollar bill.

"Oh, Dad!" She hugged him.

At Sue's house she urged, "Hurry, hurry! What if the nurse quits before we get there?"

Sue kept on combing her hair. "Relax. I think she's on duty until about one or two o'clock in the afternoon."

On the short walk to Main Street, Katie John kept touching her left earlobe. Soon there'd be a hole in it; it would never be the same again. Instead of screwing an earring onto her ear, that symbol of beauty would be inserted into her flesh and become a part of her. The palms of her hands felt damp.

"Does it hurt much?" she asked Sue.

"No. It's only like a sharp pinch. She takes a little gun instrument and shoots the post through your ear."

"Ugh."

"Really, it doesn't hurt at all after the first day."

"Huh!" Katie hadn't thought about her ears hurting for even a day. However, maybe it was right to make some sacrifice in order to change herself.

The girls crossed Main Street to the mall and wended their way through the haphazard traffic in the parking lot. The mall, opened only last spring, was a popular attraction to people in the little farming villages back in the hills as well as to the townsfolk. Katie John could remember how the lower end of Main Street had looked when she'd first moved to Barton's Bluff. The street had been lined with three-story brick buildings whose upper windows were tall and arched, with stone carvings over the arches. Granted, some of the buildings had been empty, but there had been a special old-river-town look to the street. The mall didn't look like anything. It was just a one-story sprawl of a building that, with its parking lot, covered two square blocks.

Inside, the girls hurried along a wide hallway thronged with people. Sue paused to say hi to Lou Bee, who was moseying along with some girls, and then to look at the display of winter clothing in a shop window. Katie kept pulling her on.

"Later!"

The nurse was still at the jewelry store. She had just finished piercing the ears of a young woman, who was grimacing and saying "Ow." Katie John resolved she would "scorn to yell." One last time she felt her left earlobe in its original state, before the nurse dabbed antiseptic on it.

"Now then—what's your name?—Katie John, sit very still and focus your eyes on that poster." Talking all the time, the woman felt Katie's earlobes and put little dots on them with a marker. "It won't exactly hurt, but you can expect to feel a short burn. It's important you hold steady. Don't jerk your head away when you feel the burn. Remember, don't pull away, and it's all over in a second."

While the nurse talked behind her, Katie John looked around to see what she was doing. She was loading gold studs and clips in a gray metal gun that looked like a stapler. What's more, it looked scary.

"No, don't look at this." The nurse hid the gun behind her, laughing a little. "Focus your eyes on the poster."

Katie set her teeth so she wouldn't yell. Sue nodded and smiled encouragingly, and Katie smiled back around her set teeth. She heard the nurse step up behind her, and she felt the pressure of the gun against her ear. At the stinging dart, her eyes popped wide open, yet it was over so quickly she barely winced. The other ear—*zing*—and it was done. Her ears were pierced. For the rest of her livelong life.

"Let me see!"

The lady handed her a mirror. "Looks just fine, Katie. Both holes going in the same direction!"

Katie John moved her head to one side, then to the other, to see the gold posts in her ears, making for the first time that slow feminine movement of studying oneself in a mirror. The little gold studs showed up nicely against her brown hair. In fact, Katie thought, the earrings looked so pretty on her it was as if her ears hadn't been complete before.

"I like it!"

She touched her ears and felt the tiny gold clips on the backs of the lobes. They didn't hurt, but they were beginning to feel hot, and she was glad. The sensation proved she'd done something to change herself and become more—romantical.

"Oh, Katie, you look just darling." Sue confirmed it.

"I should have done it when you did," Katie said in a rush of feeling, "so we could have done it together."

The nurse told her to rotate the posts four times a day and handed Katie a bottle of antiseptic to squirt on her ears.

"Wear the studs two to four weeks until the tissue heals, before you put on any other earrings, and always wear gold—"

"What!"

But what about the long dangly earrings at the dance just a week off?

"But a whole week off," she begged, "can't I wear some other earrings just for one evening?"

The nurse shook her head. "Not a good idea." Other earrings could move in the hole, irritating the unhealed tissue, she explained. "And if your ears swell, you might not be able to get the posts back in."

"Oh—gol-lee!"

Of all rotten things! Why hadn't Sue told her? Maybe she'd just wear dangly earrings anyway, and take her chances.

Bitter with disappointment, she shook her head at the babyish little earrings the jeweler showed her. Katie John hung over the jewelry case studying ear-

rings until even Sue grew impatient. The ones Katie
liked best cost way too much, but finally she chose
a pair that would hang long and curve backward in
scrolls. She held the earrings against her ears in
front of a mirror and approved the sweeping effect.

"I'll take these!"

The jeweler sighed, shrugged, smiled and took
her money.

When the girls left the shop and wandered
through the branching corridors of the mall toward
the Pizza Hut, they kept seeing people they knew.
Howard Bunch and some of the guys were lounging
on a bench by the stone fountain, which already had
ceased working and was full of candy wrappers and
cigarette butts. Katie John shook back her hair to
show her ears as she stopped to say hello. But just
then Howard began to wrestle with Pete, and they
didn't notice her ears.

The girls in the drugstore noticed, however. Priscilla, Betsy Ann and Lou Bee were in there getting
samples of perfume put on their wrists at a perfume
demonstration.

Sue said, "Look what Katie's done!"

The girls looked at Katie John's ears and *ooo*ed.

"That's sweet, Katie John," Priscilla said. "You're
going to love having pierced ears. I've had my ears
pierced since I was four."

Naturally.

Back in the central thoroughfare of the mall,
Katie saw the back of Ramon wandering along, then

Sammy, then the cheerleader Jackie Peterson with two guys.

"What's happening?" she asked Sue. "How come all these kids are here?"

"Oh, lots of them hang out in the mall on Saturdays. You know, eat, go to the movie. It's just something to do."

The social aspects of the shopping mall had escaped Katie. Usually on Saturdays she was either cleaning house or doing something with Edwin. With a twinge, she wondered if he was hunting geodes. Last Saturday, too, she'd been too busy to go down to the creek with him. She thought about last Saturday and the old-maid sisters and their house-pinched life, such a contrast to this thronging, shopper-hustling life in the mall.

Along with the racketing sound of music, Jason and Chuck emerged from a record-and-tape shop. Katie John sucked in her breath. She shook her hair back from her ears.

"Hi, Jason, Chuck."

"Hi. Hey!" Jason added, as Katie touched her ear with a seemingly casual finger. "You get your ears pierced? Or have you been wearing those all along?"

"I just now had it done."

"Nice!" Jason gave her that intent look of his. "I thought I would have noticed before."

That was better! Katie John's chest felt full enough with satisfaction to burst. Her ears throbbed a little, and it was worth it!

"See you." Jason and Chuck moved away.

Sue wanted to try on some winter clothes. By the time she and Katie got to the Pizza Hut, Jason and Chuck were standing by a booth in which Trish Hardwicke was sitting with some girls. Everybody said hi. Nobody said anything about Katie John's earrings.

Instead, "Oh, Katie," Trish added in her cool voice, "is the kazoo band going to play at the Homecoming Dance?"

The other girls laughed, and Jason looked at her. Katie John flushed. "No!"

She tried to shove past Chuck to get away, and her arm knocked against Trish's water glass. Trish slid out of the booth in time to escape the oncoming flood. She didn't snarl at Katie, though.

She only laughed, saying, "Good grief, Grace!"

That was the maddening thing about Trish. She never lost her poise—except for the time the balloon had dropped toward the river.

"You going to the show?" Jason asked Trish.

"No." She hooked her bag out of the booth. "I have a golf lesson, and I'd better get out in front, because Mum will be waiting."

Jason and Chuck added themselves to a noisy bunch of boys in a back booth, and Katie John tried not to get caught watching them.

After she and Sue had eaten, it was time for the movie, also housed in the mall. That afternoon's film was a horror show, *The Virginia Creeper.* At the end of it, there was to be a drawing for door prizes. Anyone who had spent ten dollars or more that day in the shopping mall could have a chance at a prize by writing his name on the receipt and dropping it in a box. Katie's receipt from the jewelry store was for more than eighteen dollars, so she fished it out of the sack, which she had carefully stowed away in her purse. For a moment she looked at the little white box that held the earrings of beauty.

Then she studied the prizes ranged around the theater lobby. Dishes, a carpet sweeper, perfume, skateboards, records—

"I'd take the perfume," said Sue.

"Yes, I guess so," Katie agreed. She couldn't see herself on a skateboard in the new image she wanted to create.

The theater was dark, modern and fairly clean— and filled with milling people. Most of the moviegoers were junior high kids, and they kept moving around, changing seats. Katie John and Sue picked a spot on the side. Just as the picture came on the screen there was a rustling in the row behind, and turning, Katie saw Jason and Chuck sit down behind them.

"Figured you girls needed a little protection, in case it gets too scary," Jason said, grinning.

Katie loved it when Jason grinned. He hardly ever did.

She looked at the screen, her heart thumping.

Jason had chosen to sit behind her.

The movie was about a vine that went on a killing rampage. The Virginia Creeper was a plant that looked like poison ivy and put out little sucker-tendrils to climb up walls of houses. Then a mad scientist, for some unexplained reason, sprayed his vine with a potion that gave the Creeper an evil intelligence, and the plant began to go wild. For another unexplained reason, the Virginia Creeper began to swarm up the brick walls of old houses and seep in the windows and strangle people.

At first the movie was kind of scary, with eerie music and slow camera pans to something you just knew was going to be awful. Sue clutched Katie, going "Ooo," and Chuck reached to pat her on the head. "There, there, little one." At the point when the ordinary vine was about to turn into an Evil Thing, Katie John's breath got short, and when it turned its awful head to the camera, she shrieked. All the girls in the theater screamed, too. She felt Jason patting her shoulder, "There, there—"

But Katie John began to laugh. The faked-up Thing looked too ridiculous to be scary. You could see the skinny legs of a guy in black tights at the center of the mass of reaching vines, manipulating the greenery with his arms, and the awful head actually looked like an owl's face.

"Oh, hee hee," Katie giggled.

Some of the girls kept screaming, but some people were laughing, and some of the boys were yell-ing to urge the Creeper on to its evil deeds.

By camera trickery, the vines crawling up the side of an old house looked real and horrible. But in the room, threatening the beautiful young girl, the Virginia Creeper was the owl-faced guy in his clump of shrubbery. Music intensified as he crept up behind the girl, and then the Creeper spoke.

"Ah'll git mah revenge!"

The Virginia Creeper had a southern accent.

Katie John went into hysterics. She laughed so hard as the scene developed that she had to double over to relieve her aching sides.

"What's the matter with you?" Sue exclaimed. "The Creeper is horrible! It's strangling her!"

"I can't help it," Katie gasped, wiping tears from her eyes.

She glanced back at Jason, but he was only watching the screen with a rather solemn look on his face. At her glance, he looked at her, shaking his head slightly without changing expression.

After that, Katie John tried not to laugh at the ridiculous movie, and the more she tried not to, the more giggling fits she went into.

When it was all over, and the Creeper had strangled the mad scientist, Sue said, "Honestly, Katie John! It wasn't all that funny!"

Katie panted as if she'd run a three-mile race. "I can't help it," she squeaked, weak from laughing.

From behind, Chuck said, "We'd better walk these girls home. I don't think Katie John can make it on her own."

As the lights came on, a man came out on the stage with the box of receipts, and Katie remembered about the door prize. An usher lugged the prizes onto the stage. There was more suspense to the drawing ceremony than there'd been to the movie, the way the man dragged it out. Bit by bit, a teenaged girl got the dishes; some little kid won the records; a grown-up lady won the skateboard, and when everybody laughed, she called she was giving it to her son. There was still the perfume, and Katie John sat up intent, as the man put his hand in the box again. She could wear the perfume at the dance. However, the man called out some boy's name, and she flopped back, shrugging.

"Come on, let's go," she said to Sue.

"No, wait. There's still a few prizes."

And so, on the very last drawing, the man called out, "Katie John Tucker!"

"Wow!" She jumped up.

The only prize left was the carpet sweeper.

Of all the dumb things! A lot of the kids were laughing. Katie couldn't look at Jason. Nevertheless, she went forward to receive the thing. At least she'd won something. And actually, the carpet sweeper would be handy for hasty cleanups of the carpets in the long hallways at her house. Everybody clapped and hoorahed and got up to leave.

Katie John tried to push the carpet sweeper up the aisle through the crowd, but that was awkward, and besides, she didn't want to collect all the trash on the floor into her new sweeper. She picked it up, and that was awkward, too. Carpet sweepers weren't designed to be handled in any way except scooted across a floor.

Outside the theater, Sue, Chuck and Jason were waiting for her in the mall.

Smiling, Jason said, "What are you going to do with that thing?"

"Sweep, I guess." To take Jason's attention away from any possibly humorous aspects of the situation, Katie John shook her hair back from her ears, saying, "My ears feel really hot now, but it's worth it."

"They look swell," Jason said, and Katie's face felt hot, as well.

Then she felt silly, pushing the carpet sweeper over the floor of the mall as they walked toward the exit. Sue, Chuck and Jason moved ahead of her. At the door to the parking lot, she picked up the sweeper by the handle and carried it, but it was heavier than she'd expected. She tried balancing the long handle over her shoulder, but that didn't work either. Holding the thing crossways in her arms, like a very long baby, Katie John dodged cars and caught up with her group.

Across Main Street she set the pesky sweeper down and pushed it up the sidewalk. Jason walked beside her except one step ahead. Talk about ridiculous horror movies! For the first time in her life, a boy was walking her home from a movie, and she had to be pushing a carpet sweeper!

It began to rattle with all the pebbles and junk it was picking up. Probably the stuff was gumming up the brush, too.

Somebody honked a car horn and yelled out the window, "Hey, cutie! Sweep the gutter, too!"

Chuck laughed, and Sue made little worried sounds. Jason stared at the top of a building. Katie hoisted the contraption so the sweeper box rested on her hip and the handle stuck up in the air.

"Here, I'll carry that thing for you," Jason said.

Gladly, yet with shame, Katie John relinquished the sweeper. How could anybody pay attention to her pierced ears, when she was shoving a carpet sweeper up the sidewalk? Having her ears pierced wasn't enough. Besides *looking* attractive, she'd have to change the way she behaved.

Katie scuffed her toes along beside silent Jason. The trouble was, she wasn't sure she wanted to change. After all, taking the carpet sweeper was perfectly logical. If she had to go through life being careful not to do anything that might turn out funny . . . she wasn't sure she wanted to walk such a tightrope.

7

Won't You Dance with Me?

At home Katie John gave the carpet sweeper a vicious shove so it zoomed and clattered down the length of the hallway.

"Here's a stupid present!" she called to her mother, who was back in the kitchen.

Mrs. Tucker was glad about the carpet sweeper. Dad was back in the kitchen, too. Katie John rotated the gold posts in her ears, wincing, and both her parents were properly appreciative of how lovely she looked with pierced ears. For once Dad didn't make any jokes. Actually, he looked a little sad.

Mrs. Tucker reminded her pierce-eared princess that the damp sheets still needed to be run through the electric ironer. So Katie John went down to the basement to get that done before supper.

Sitting at the old-fashioned ironer, she could hear faint sounds of the television set in the Hitchens apartment. Then they grew louder when Mrs. Hitchens opened the door and came out to visit. She left the door open, so the blare of the television set mingled with the drone of her voice.

"Gonna get crowded in there. Don't know how we'll manage." She plopped down on an old couch that was handy for folding stacks of laundry.

"How's that?" Katie wished the poor little woman would go back into her rooms with her husband and shut the door.

"Husband's nephew's coming. Anyways, you'll have some young company in this old house."

"Oh?"

"Yuh, Delby, he's a little older'n you, I'd guess. Fourteen or rising fifteen. Seems he got into a little trouble down home at Joeville, and—"

Oh, my heavens, Katie John thought, turning off. All she needed was another boy around to think about. Once before a renter had come with a child, but Buster had been only a little boy for her to baby-sit.

Ironing done, she began to gather the laundry into baskets to take upstairs.

"How nice," she said, trying to be polite.

"Yuh," Mrs. Hitchens said, getting up, "he'll be here tomorrow, so I guess you'll meet him."

"Swell!"

As Katie escaped toward the basement stairs, the

woman said, "See you got your ears pierced. Your ears look red. Better cool 'em off with a piece of ice."

"Yes, I will." The woman wasn't so bad, after all.

Sunday afternoon it rained, so Katie John and Sue practiced dancing at Sue's house. At least, Katie thought, she'd be able to dance with Sue, even if no boy asked her. Probably most of the seventh-grade boys wouldn't know how to dance, anyway. She got the giggles as she pictured Howard and Edwin practicing dancing together. Of course, Jason, being a year older, should know how to dance.

That night, eating supper with her parents, Katie heard her dog howling behind the house in the rain. She ran downstairs to bring Heavenly Spot through the cellar so his feet wouldn't be so wet and muddy by the time he got upstairs. Hurrying through the laundry room, she stopped abruptly. A boy was sitting on the old couch. He was shoving a magazine under a stack of magazines beside him.

"Who—? Oh."

"Hello-dah! Name's Delby Hitchens. What's yours?"

She told him, staring. She could believe he'd gotten into a little trouble down at Joeville. One of his lower teeth was missing, and that, with the way his dark blond hair lopped down over his eyes, gave him a rakish look.

Katie John shivered, hunching her shoulders.

"Yeah, it's cold down in this hole," Delby said.

"Your dad said he'd turn the furnace on tomorrow, if it keeps on raining. He said I could have the job of taking care of the furnace."

Heavenly Spot howled and scraped at the cellar door, so Katie went to let him in. The grateful beagle reared up and planted his muddy front paws on her pants, then ran to the boy, as if they'd already gotten acquainted.

"You know what I'm gonna do with the money your old man pays me for the furnace work? Gonna buy me a motor-sickle!"

"Yeah?" Katie doubted her dad would pay him enough for that. Still, "Could I ride on it?"

"Sure." He grinned at her, his brown eyes intimate. "You can hold onta me. You're kinda cute."

Feeling her face get red, Katie John bent down to swipe the dog's feet on an old piece of carpet. "You going to be here long?" She wasn't sure she wanted him to be, with his takeover ways, adventure magazines scattered on the couch—and who-knows-what kind of magazine shoved underneath. He looked at least fifteen.

"Dunno. See how I like your high-class school." He leaned his head back on his arms, eyeing her. "What grade you in?"

"Seventh."

"Huh! Chickie-babe. I'm in ninth. Izzat the same school?"

"Yes." Right away Katie John decided she'd leave early in the morning, so she wouldn't get involved

99

in walking to school with him. Not until she knew better what she thought of him. "Gotta go. Come on, Spot."

Monday at school Katie had just caught up with Edwin in the hallway to show him her pierced ears when Delby came out of a classroom.

"Hey, chickie-babe," he said, "sit with me in the cafeteria this noon. Help me get acquainted, okay?"

Edwin stared after him as Delby swaggered down the hall. "Who's that?"

"Oh, a guy who came to live with the people in our basement," Katie John said, frowning a little. "I'm not sure I like him. He's awfully—"

She couldn't finish it, and after a moment, Edwin said, "Yeah, I can see he is!"

"Anyway, look. I got my ears pierced." She held her hair back from her ears.

Edwin looked at the gold studs. "Huh. Why did you do that?"

"Well— Don't you like how they look?"

"I don't know." Edwin studied her, his eyes narrowed, his brow slightly wrinkled. "Makes you look different."

Katie John laughed. "That's the point." When Edwin only sniffed and walked on, she went with him, adding, "I did it Saturday, and that's why I couldn't come to hunt geodes. Did you find any more?"

"No, I had to help my dad mow the grounds one

more time before winter." He wouldn't smile at her, and she didn't know what he was thinking.

At noon Edwin sat with some of the boys at a table clear across the lunchroom. Katie John sat with Sue and Bob, and sure enough, pretty soon Delby came and sat down by her.

"You shoulda showed me where this school is at! Already I'm in trouble because I got here late." He laughed, and his voice was too loud even for the clattery cafeteria.

Priscilla and Lou Bee brought their trays to the table, obviously to learn who the new boy was. Immediately Delby began to kid with the girls, and although Priscilla's mouth tucked in with disdain, Lou Bee cocked her head at him, eyes alert. Katie John saw Jason glancing at them from another table.

The next day in cooking class she was gratified to hear Jason ask, "Who was that guy with you yesterday?"

She was becoming more sure she didn't like Delby Hitchens very well. Still, maybe it wouldn't hurt for Jason to see an older boy paying attention to her.

By Thursday afternoon of Homecoming Week the fight posters, made in art class, had been hung in the hallways; the gymnasium had been decorated for the dance; the football teams, cheerleaders and kazoo band had practiced vigorously; and a token amount of classwork had been done. It stopped rain-

101

ing Thursday, too. After school Katie John biked out to the cemetery creek with Edwin to search again for geodes.

It was a good thing Edwin and Mr. Jones had cut the grass earlier, because the wind and rain had brought down a drift of glistening brown oak leaves on the grass and gravestones. There was a fresh damp smell to the hilly cemetery, and the green and russet leaves still on the trees shone new-washed. As always, a mourning dove called *hoo, hoo* in the quiet. Coasting down the narrow roadway to the creek, Katie John saw it was running with a bit of water again. She and Edwin got shovels from the toolshed and jumped down the muddy banks to the rocky edges of the stream.

Katie looked at the gravestones on the steep little hills above the creek, then at the water running over the rocks in the middle. What if she or Edwin found more than geodes?

"All this rain—do the bones ever get washed down into the creek?"

"Oh, Katie John!" Edwin snorted a laugh. "Believe me, all the bones are safe in their boxes!"

They went downstream, Katie on one side, Edwin on the other, poking their shovels here and there at promising rocks. Katie John slipped on a wet rock, then looked at it more closely. It was a rough round gray stone about the size of a grapefruit.

"Hey, I think I found one! It's not very big, but it's definitely a geode!"

Edwin hefted it. "Yeah!" he agreed. "Good!"

He tossed it up onto the bank, and Katie noted that her geode was by a standing tombstone that read ALDRICH. Now to find a bigger geode. She touched her left ear stud for luck, a habit she'd gotten into that week. Her ears didn't burn or hurt at all by then, and she'd been debating whether to go ahead and wear the dangly earrings to the dance.

"I still wish you'd go to the dance," she muttered to Edwin, as she investigated a rock embedded in exposed tree roots in the bank.

"Huh. Say, I want to ask you something."

Katie John abandoned the rock and looked at him. Edwin seldom wanted to ask her anything.

"How come you're hanging around with all these guys all of a sudden?"

Edwin looked so seriously at her that Katie fumbled with her shovel.

"All what guys? I can't help it if that dumb Delby moved into our house."

"Yeah, well— But I heard you went to the movie with Jason Schreiber last Saturday."

"I did not! Who told you that? Lou Bee? He and Chuck just happened to sit behind us, and then when I won the carpet sweeper, Jason helped carry it home." Katie turned back to the rock in the tree roots, because she felt a guilty look come over her face.

"Huh." Edwin moved on down the creek.

Above, a white marble gravestone took on a rosy

hue in the setting sunlight, and the dove called a final *hooo*. It was such a contrast to the commercial bustle of the shopping mall.

Katie John offered, "I don't see how those kids can stand to hang around a shopping center every Saturday, when they could be out doing something. I'd a lot rather be here."

"I'll say!" Edwin, turning, gave her a quick smile and stretched his shoulders as he looked up at the trees. "Yes, in a week or two we ought to go out to Wildcat Glen and see whether the walnuts are ready."

Friday after school the Junior Varsity team won its football game, and Katie John, caught up in the excitement of it all, pranced and wheezed in the kazoo band. Saturday afternoon the ninth-grade team lost its game with the Catholic school team, but that didn't lessen one whit the eagerness of everyone for the dance that night.

Right after supper Katie John went upstairs to prepare. First, a bath, then clean clothes from the skin out. Instead of wearing pants, she put on a green tunic-type dress that made her eyes look more green. Then, before the arched mirror over the little marble-topped dresser, she took the gold studs out of her ears for the first time. Leaning close to the mirror, she studied the holes and decided they looked perfectly well healed.

Carefully she inserted the gold wire through the

104

left hole, tilting her head to watch the effect of the long golden earring. Oh, yes! The other one . . . She moved her head to see the golden scrolls sweep against her brown hair. The girl in the mirror . . . *I never saw you before.*

What was that on her chin? A pimple! Of all times to start a pimple—that's what she got for eating all those cookies lately. Katie went back to the bathroom and rummaged in the drawers for her mother's face makeup. She smudged some tan cream over the pink lump, and the makeup disguised it pretty well.

Now for the perfume. Up two steps out of the back wing and down the long flight of front stairs Katie hurried to her parents' bedroom across the hall from the parlor. As she ran down the steps, the earrings swung slightly to her rhythm, and she liked the new feeling, the reminder of femininity. The gold posts hadn't moved at all, and a lot of the time she'd forgotten they were there. Katie found her mother's best perfume and dabbed it on her wrists, behind her ears—

Oh, oh. Her earlobes were beginning to feel a little warm. Very gently Katie pulled on the left earring and felt a small twinge. The tissue must not be totally healed. The movement of the gold wires was irritating her ears. If just running down the stairs made the earrings move, what would her earlobes be like after an evening of dancing?

"Oh, darn!"

It wasn't the pain she minded; she'd probably forget that at the dance. But what if her ears swelled up so she couldn't get the posts back in? If she had to wait a few days to get the posts in, the holes might grow shut. Yet tonight was the reason she'd wanted the dangly earrings.

"Darn, darn, darn!" Katie trudged back up the stairs. Just below the top step she stopped, trying to decide what to do. At last she kicked the top step and went on back to her room. If she wanted to wear dangles in the future, she'd better take them out now. Anyway, she tried to console herself, if her ears got red and swollen at the dance, she wouldn't look lovely, anyway. Anyway . . . anyway, she smelled good.

Katie John managed to get the gold studs back into her earlobes, got her bag and ran down the stairs again. Delby was waiting in the front hall.

"I'll walk you to the dance," he said, grinning up at her.

Katie John teetered on the bottom step in dismay. How could she expect Jason to ask her to dance, if she arrived with another boy? Was Delby planning to stick to her like glue? Of course, he was kind of good-looking and tall, but—

"Well, I'm going with Sue Halsey, but—I guess you can walk over with us, if you want."

"Sure, be glad to take two little girls to the dance." He grinned. "Course, I can't promise to bring you home. Gotta look this situation over."

Katie John snorted. What an ego!

Long as it had taken Katie to get ready, Sue was taking even longer, still trying to decide what to wear. So they got to the dance fashionably late. In the gymnasium there was no problem of Jason seeing her arrive with another boy. There was such a mass of people milling around, it would be a wonder if he saw her at all. Very few kids were dancing to the loud music yet, but they lined the walls of the gym and swarmed up and down the floor from the refreshment tables at one end to the pool tables at the other end. Some boy hailed Delby, and gratefully Katie saw him peel off. She and Sue went to stand with some other girls along the wall and assess the situation.

Girls, more than boys, were dancing, although some of the older boys had partners. Katie saw Lou Bee and Ramon bounce past. In a cluster near the refreshment tables stood Trish Hardwicke, looking positively beautiful, with her long brown hair piled up in an enchanting way. Katie John couldn't see Jason anywhere. What if—her heart suddenly sank—what if he didn't even come?

"Let's walk down toward the pool tables," she told Sue. She couldn't see who all was down there.

The boys down there proved to include Howard, who called, "Come on, Katie, shoot a few with us."

She shook her head. She hadn't come to the dance, all feminine, to shoot pool with the guys. She noticed Priscilla and Betsy Ann weren't fooling with cue sticks; they were watching and making cute remarks about the boys' shots.

There he was! Over on the other side of the gym, Jason was sauntering up toward the punch-and-cookies tables.

The music stopped and began again, playing a popular tune with a good beat.

"Come on, let's dance," Sue said.

At first, Katie John felt nervous and awkward at dancing, but more kids got out on the floor, so she and Sue weren't conspicuous. Dancing with Sue, Katie saw Jason with a paper cup in his hand, talking to some guys. Standing on the sidelines with Sue, Katie saw Jason talking to Trish. Standing on the sidelines while Bob danced with Sue, Katie saw Jason dancing with Trish.

And he was a good dancer, too. Katie John looked away.

She stood on the sidelines waiting for some boy to ask her to dance. At last, Ramon did. They got along all right except when they bumped into Jason, who was dancing with some older girl. Then Ramon danced with Sue, and Bob danced with Katie. She couldn't see Jason anywhere, and there was a slightly sick feeling in her stomach as she footed it along with Bob and tried to talk.

When Bob and Sue went up to get some punch, Katie trailed along with them. The drink seemed tasteless, but her parched throat was thankful for liquid.

Behind her, Jason said, "You want to dance, Katie?"

"Oh!" She turned, punch lurching in the cup. "Sure, I guess so." She set the cup back on the table.

Taking her lightly by the hand, Jason led Katie John out onto the floor. The music was the kind where people danced without touching each other, and it was faster than Katie was used to. Bobbing opposite Jason, she struggled to catch up with the beat. She was so awkward! Tears pricked her eyes as she tried to smile at Jason.

"Go like this." He took her by the waist and clicked his tongue to the beat, "Tck, tck," then swung her out again.

He was so kind!

And his face looked so cool and easy as he danced.

When the number was over, there was an intermission. Would they stand around together?

"Better see if my punch cup is still there," Katie muttered.

"Yeah. See you." Jason drifted off.

Katie John got more punch and found Sue and Bob to stand with. When the music started again, she saw Jason dancing with Trish, then some other girl, then Trish. Trish's hair was toppling down, and she looked even more pretty than elegant. Katie John touched the gold stud in her left ear. Her throat felt tight.

She was about to wander down to the pool tables

again, while Sue and Bob were dancing, when Delby Hitchens loomed up.

"C'mon, Katie, let's go!"

"Well, but—" she began, but Delby hauled her out onto the floor.

He started gyrating to the music opposite her. Katie John gyrated, too, although she realized she certainly wasn't doing what Delby was. He was dancing a kind of syncopated stomp, his heavy boots going *ka-clop, ka-clop*.

"Watch out, don't stomp on my foot!" Katie gasped. "What are you *doing*?"

"Ever'body dances like this down at Joeville. This is the Joeville Stomp!"

Delby grabbed Katie's hand and swung her around so she nearly broke her arm. Then he clutched her close and charged down the floor, stomping. Everybody had to get out of their way, because they were like a locomotive coming. Katie John's face felt red and stiff. Even Howard, moving along ponderous as an elephant with Priscilla, grinned and shook his head at them. Blessedly, she couldn't see Jason anywhere. That was partly because she shut her eyes in shame when Delby reversed and charged back up the floor. When the music stopped abruptly, and her eyes popped open, she saw they'd cleaved a path through the dancers.

Also she saw Jason and Trish, who had been dancing together. Trish looked at her and said something to Jason, smiling. Jason looked at her with no expression on his face.

"Hey, Katie, that was great! Let's go again!"

Katie John pulled away from Delby. "No, I'm tired."

Not only tired, she realized, but panting and sweating, and her face burned like fire. The perfume smelled strong, brought out by her perspiration. What an awful spectacle she was!

She got clear away from everybody. Hurrying to the rest room, she washed the sweat off and held wet paper towels to her hot face until it calmed down some. However, in the mirror her face still looked blotchy, and the pimple fairly glowed. She got her chin under the faucet and ran cold water until her chin felt frozen. She wasn't going out until Delby Hitchens had found somebody else to make a fool of.

When at last Katie John cautiously entered the gym again, she studied the crowd until she spotted Delby safely occupied at a pool table with some older boys. She drank another cup of punch, standing apart from the kids around the table, who were all strangers. Everybody she knew was dancing.

Later, Sue found her, and they danced together, but Katie John couldn't enjoy it. The heart had gone out of her. Jason didn't come near her again. She was thankful when the dance ended.

"Come on," Sue said, "I've got to go to the rest room before we leave."

Half the girls at the dance, it seemed, had to go to the rest room. They swarmed the line of toilets and jockeyed for position in front of the mirrors, where they washed, put on lipstick and brushed out their hair. Katie John stood back against the wall and waited for Sue. Everybody was talking about where they were going "after" and with whom.

Priscilla Simmons: "Howard and Pete are taking me and Betsy Ann to—"

Lou Bee: "Ramon says they've got a special at—"

Trish Hardwicke, pinning her hair back into a lovely washerwoman's mop: "Jason and Chuck said they'd—"

Katie John pushed out of the rest room to wait outside for Sue. Probably even if she had worn long dangly earrings it wouldn't have made any difference. She held her cold hands to her hot cheeks.

And then when Sue came out, she said, "Bob and I and Lou Bee and Ramon are going down to the Pizza Hut, and you come too, okay?"

"I—no." Katie shook her head. "I'm awfully tired. I think I'd better go on home."

Sue protested, but when they came outdoors on the steps, Katie John was even more sure. Lots of the boys were out there, waiting for the girls, and everybody was pairing off. Boys' faces looking up for their girls, Jason's face, not watching for her—

" 'Bye, Sue." Katie turned to hurry away in the dark.

"Hey, wait up, Katie!" a voice bellowed. "I'll walk ya home."

Delby Hitchens, of course.

"No, I—" she said desperately. "Really, I—"

"Sure, you're going my way!" He grasped her elbow to march her away.

Katie John had a glimpse of Jason. He was grinning. Not only did she want to die, she felt as if something inside her had. Her mouth felt all sucked in, pouty. *Baby, baby, baby . . .*

Katie stretched her mouth into a grin, laughing past Jason. "C'mon, Delby, let's go!"

8

The Kissed Club

Sunday afternoon Katie John paid a call on Miss Esther Collingwood to get better acquainted with the old lady and her dove. Esther told tales of the olden days in Barton's Bluff, and by the end of the visit, Gulliver was trusting enough to peck birdseed from Katie's hand. It soothed her to think about something and someone else besides boys—and herself. Monday morning Katie vowed to concentrate on nothing but schoolwork.

Therefore, it came as a shock to discover that more had gone on after the dance than she'd realized. Several of the girls, she noticed, were wearing little cardboard badges lettered *K.C.* in red. Idly she wondered what that meant, but her mind was on the essay she had to write for English. Dressing in the girls' locker room after Gym class, she saw Trish had one of those badges pinned to her shirt.

It was Priscilla who asked, "What does K.C. stand for?"

Trish smiled, glancing sideways at Priscilla. "Can't you guess?"

"Goodness, I don't know. Let's see, what begins with *K*?"

Lou Bee looked up from tying her boots. "Kitchen? Huh, not for you, Trish! Kitten?"

"Silly!" Trish laughed. "*Kissed!* It stands for *Kissed Club.*"

"What!"

The girls stared and laughed, and Trish was the center of attention. The brown-eyed cheerleader, who also was wearing K.C., nodded, dimpling.

"Some of us were talking Sunday," Trish explained, "and we got to kidding around, and we decided to do this. Everybody who's been kissed can wear the badge."

"Oh, well, gee—"

"Trish, you mean really you—"

Through the girls' titillated talk, Katie John burst, "Oh, how vulgar!"

"Yes," Trish agreed gaily, "but it's fun."

Katie thought Trish would have been too sophisticated for such behavior, yet there she was giggling, eyes lively, same as the other girls.

Who? Jason or Chuck?

That business earlier with Sue about S.W., Some-

115

body Wonderful, was babyish compared to this. The *in* girls were always way ahead of her.

"So what does this club do? Are you going to have meetings?" Katie John snorted in derision.

"As a matter of fact, we are," Trish said. "Friday night everybody who can wear a K.C. badge is meeting at my house, and we're going to compare notes on which boy kisses the best."

"Oh, ugh!" Katie John was so disgusted her throat felt thick. "Kiss and tell, huh?"

Trish giggled. "Gotcha! Oh, Katie John, you take everything so seriously. No, we're not really going to do that. However, I am having a party Friday night after the game, and you're invited, even without a badge."

The party was for the football team, the cheerleaders, the kazoo band and a few others. Priscilla was invited, too.

"Thanks, but I don't know if I can—" Katie turned away, because Trish wasn't listening, anyway.

She was saying, "The fun part will be to see which girls put on a K.C. badge."

Katie John felt sick at her stomach. Her revulsion was so great she couldn't think about anything but the Kissed Club. The next day she watched girls' left chests to see if a K.C. badge would appear. There, a little red one on Betsy Ann, on Priscilla Simmons— you'd think *she'd* be too ladylike for that junk.

Naturally, the next thing to wonder was who had

kissed the girls? Had Howard Bunch kissed Priscilla? Had Jason kissed Trish? Katie's chest felt squeezed. And were the girls lying with their badges?

Oh, it was rotten stuff to be thinking about!

Walking home with Sue, Katie exclaimed, "Did you ever see anything so cheap?"

Sue only smiled. "I could wear one of those badges, if I wanted to. Bob kissed me when we were six years old."

"But you don't—now—?"

"No." Sue's face got pink.

Katie John kicked at the leaves on the sidewalk and sent them rattling. If there was any chance Jason still might like her, despite the carpet-sweeper episode, despite Delby at the dance, then someday he might— But it ought to be—

"Kissing ought to be private!" she declared. "The way the girls chased boys last year, I thought *that* was the little life! If this is the normal way to act, I may just resign from the human race!"

The thing was, the girls' badges provided a natural reason for teasing and talking about kissing. Most of the seventh grade took to it with glee. As the fever built Wednesday, Katie John heard one teacher say to another, "My heavens! If it's this bad now, what will it be like in the spring?"

In a way, the worst was when Lou Bee appeared with a K.C. badge on her blouse. The pretty little dark girl came walking out of Shop with Edwin, laughing up to him and calling him *Eddie.* Surely, *Edwin wouldn't*— No, Katie reminded herself, Lou Bee had gone with Ramon after the dance.

At home that night, glum, minding her own business, Katie went down to the basement to fetch a fresh sack of dog food for Heavenly Spot. Sitting on the couch in the laundry room was Delby, with his stack of magazines.

"Welcome to my cave! Hey, Katie, c'mere. I wanta show you the motor-sickle in this magazine." He moved over and patted a place for her on the couch. When she only stood near to look, he pulled her down. "Siddown. See."

"Yeah, swell bike," she said without enthusiasm.

Delby began laughing. "Whoo, that K.C. business at school! I helped out one of you kiddy-girls. How about you?" He slid an arm around her. "You want a kiss?"

"Good grief, no!" Katie John jumped up.

"Sure you do." He took her hand lightly.

Katie looked at him, the daredevil sparkle in his eyes, the curve of his mouth—

"No!" She shook her hand loose. "Leave me alone!"

She went to get the sack of dog food. When she came back, Delby was smoking a cigarette.

"Okay," he said, grinning and tapping ashes on the floor, "if you don't want a kiss, do you want a drag off my cigarette?"

"Yes!" Katie John snatched it out of his hand and

threw it in the laundry tub. "Now you get out of here with your cigarettes, before you burn down our house!"

Delby kept on grinning. "Hey, you're cute when you're mad."

"I'm cute like—like your grandma's hind leg!"

The nerve of that guy! Katie hurried up the cellar stairs, her knees feeling weak. Even if his mouth did look— She didn't want it to happen that way.

Thursday a fresh crop of K.C. badges bloomed on the chests of the seventh-grade girls. They looked as if they all were wearing campaign buttons. Even Sue wore a badge.

"After all, I qualify." She shrugged at Katie's sour look.

I could have qualified, too, Katie John thought. But that wasn't the point. She went through the day extremely conscious of her undecorated bosom.

After school she went out to Edwin's house to crack open their geodes and learn what they'd found. Peaceably they worked in the garage, where they had assembled a respectable little pile of the rocks, about ten of them. Edwin had fixed a box of sand as a cushion, and in it he placed a rock about the size of a cantaloupe. With a heavy hammer he tapped on a chisel around the equator of the rock, while Katie John turned it on its bed of sand. A chip of rock flew off.

"Now watch out for my fingers! Hey!"

A crack in the rock appeared, and after another

119

tap it broke open.

"Bingo!"

The insides of the two halves were like caverns crusty with crushed glass that sparkled whiter than sunlight.

"Did you ever see anything so fresh and brilliant!" Katie exclaimed.

She and Edwin each held a half to study it in the sunset light through the open garage door. Katie John touched her finger over the shining crystals that had formed in ancient days, deposited by mineral action from water inside the rock.

"To think! These crystals have never shone in the light of day until this minute! They've been there—how long? Thousands of years?"

"I don't know, maybe millions of years. I'll have to find a book about geodes." Edwin's face was lit up, intent over his piece of geode. "And we're the first ever to see the insides of this—this hidden treasure! I feel like Balboa."

"Huh?"

"When he first laid eyes on the Pacific Ocean, discovering it. Here"—Edwin set another geode in the box of sand—"let's see what's in this one."

The adventure of discovery went on. The next geode had smooth brown bumps on the walls of its hollow, and inside another was only an oily kind of mud; but the other rocks were lined with jagged crystals like diamonds. At last, when the seventh geode proved a tough nut to crack, Edwin stopped to rest.

As if idly making conversation, he asked, "Are you going to that party at Trish Hardwicke's?"

"I don't know." Katie picked up a geode shell to study it again. "I guess I'm supposed to, because of the kazoo band, you know." She kept on looking at the geode.

"Well—I'm glad you're not wearing one of those silly badges." Edwin's voice was muffled, because he was bending over the pile of geodes, his back to her.

Katie John had the notion he cared more than he let on. Maybe she did, too.

"I'm glad you're glad—Ed." She reached down and flipped the Indian feather of yellow hair that stood up on the back of his head.

"Katie *John*!" He gave her a look of awful disgust and moved away.

She understood. Teasing was like flirting, and she wasn't supposed to flirt with a friend. Besides, at flirting she was like a dinosaur trying to do a toe dance.

Yes, she thought dismally, fingering the crystals, she and Edwin were friends, so they would just go on matter-of-fact and plod-footed.

But Edwin came back with another geode he'd found in the corner and set it down, saying, "I guess I know what's the matter with you. You want to be a member of the Kissed Club. Okay." Face determined, he approached her.

"No!" It was Katie John's turn to retreat. She shouldn't have tried to start something. She'd never know how to behave with Edwin afterward, if he kissed her.

Nevertheless, he grabbed her arm—"Edwin, no!"—and kissed her elbow a smack.

"There! Now you've been kissed, and you can wear that silly badge, if you want to." He grinned.

"Oh, Edwin!" Katie John burst out laughing. "You're—you're all right!"

Smiling, she touched the place on her elbow, as she turned back to the geodes. Nothing plod-footed about that!

Friday morning Katie decided to go to Trish's party. She'd probably hate it, but she had to see, once and for all, how Jason would act toward Trish.

Following the game after school, she went home and changed. At the last minute she went back into her room, took out the gold posts and put on the long curving earrings.

"There!" She nodded approval at the mirror. That was the courage she needed.

However, when her father drove her out to Trish's house near the Country Club, she told him anxiously, "Don't leave me here too long. Come back in two hours, okay?"

Trish's house, set under oak trees, rambled back

in an excess of richness. It certainly was big enough to accommodate the thirty or so kids swarming into it. There was a long family room with a fireplace—but no fire—a game room with a pool table, a glass garden room with an indoor swimming pool—plus, in a wing seemingly off limits to the kids, a formal living room done in grays touched with crystal.

"Gosh!" Katie John sighed.

In the family room Trish was greeting her guests, "Hi! Hi! Oh hello, Katie John. So you *could* come."

Katie found Priscilla Simmons to stand with and looked around. The bar counter between the family room and the kitchen was loaded with food: pizza, potato salad, burgers, molded fruit salads and all the trimmings.

She said to Priscilla, "I thought Trish's mother didn't cook."

"She had it catered from the Country Club." Priscilla smiled a demure little smile at Katie.

Jason was there. Casually wandering around, Katie John finally located him beside the swimming pool in the garden room. Jason and Chuck were talking with some other boys about the football game they'd just played and what they *should* have done and what they *would* have done, if so-and-so hadn't—

Katie John wandered on. She'd never been to a party like this, with boys and girls, and she didn't know many of the people. Most of them were the country-club bunch, she realized. There were no adults in sight. Priscilla and Lou Bee were in the kitchen helping Trish relay paper plates and utensils onto the counter. Katie edged her way to the kitchen, but the girls didn't need any more help. By the counter was a tub full of ice and soft-drink cans, so she took a can for something to do. She tried to talk to the kazoo-band girls, but they kept darting off to someone else. She moved her head to feel the gold dangles sway. Nobody had said anything about her earrings. In the game room, Howard Bunch was shooting pool with some of the boys, and this time Katie John would have been grateful to get into the game, so she could quit wandering around, but there were no more cue sticks.

She leaned against a wall and sipped her pop. *So what am I, a ghost at the party?* She might as well be invisible, for all anybody wanted to talk to her. So all right, she'd just be a ghost and observe what a swell country-club party was like. It was noisy with the chatter of people and music on a stereo, but mostly it looked aimless. Other than standing around, there wasn't anything to do, except play pool. She wished Jason would circulate more, but at least he wasn't talking to Trish.

Trish turned off the stereo. "All right, everybody," she called, "come and get it! Food's ready."

Somehow Howard and his buddies managed to swarm out of the pool room to be at the head of the line. Hanging back, Katie found herself with Jason, who ambled in from the garden room.

For something to say, she said, "If we'd brought our suits, we could swim."

"Yeah. That'd feel good, after the game." He glanced around, not particularly looking at her. However, he added, "You go ahead of me in the line," and that was nice of him.

"You played a good game," Katie John offered.

"Aaah, no. I don't know what was the matter with me today. Hey, Chuck, next time you hand the ball off to me, would you please—" He went back into the game discussion.

Katie John filled her plate and found a place on the floor at one side of the wide stone-faced fireplace. Nobody she knew sat near her. Priscilla and Lou Bee, Howard and Ramon, all the people she knew were already settled on the long couches angling around the empty fireplace. Jason took his plate to an armchair on the other side of the fireplace, and pretty soon Trish perched on the arm with a piece of pizza and a can of pop. The girl looked so easily possessive, sitting there over Jason, chatting to him, throwing out light remarks to the others.

Chewing morosely on a hamburger, Katie glanced at her watch. Another hour before she could go home, before her father would be there to pick her up.

Jason didn't seem to look at Trish in any special way.

"Oh, Katie, I've been meaning to ask," Trish

called, "who was that guy you went with after the dance?"

Katie John's mouth was full of burger. As she chewed to get it down, some of the kids looked at her, and she felt her face getting hot.

"Oh, he's just somebody who's living at my house for a while," she mumbled. "Name's Delby."

Trish laughed. "Delby! I believe it. Country sticks out on him a mile." She dipped her head to Jason, and her long hair shielded whatever she whispered to him.

Katie felt tied to her plate. She wished she hadn't put so much food on it. Eating and eating, she planned that when she'd worked her way through enough stuff so she could politely throw away the rest, she'd go outside and—

Trish, who had hopped up, came back with a bottle, saying, "Hey, while we're all around the fireplace, let's play a game. Let's play Truth or Dare!"

The boys all groaned and laughed, and the girls all laughed and chattered.

"Trust Trish!"

"And whoever hasn't joined the Kissed Club can—"

Katie John tried to get her legs untangled to get out of there. She'd never played Truth or Dare, but Sue had talked about it. It always ended up with telling which boy you liked best and kissing and maybe even having to take off some piece of clothing. Some of the boys were getting up, too.

126

"No fair leaving," Trish said. "Whoever leaves is chicken."

"Ah *ha*!" The kids were laughing at each other.

Katie saw Jason glancing over at her. She sat back down with her plate.

Trish got the kids in back to sit on the floor between the couches and chairs so there was a rough three-quarter circle facing the fireplace. She inserted herself into the circle.

"Okay, Jason," she said, "you're on one end, so you start."

"Ah, Trish!"

Jason often acted so withdrawn Katie thought he would refuse. But he got up and squatted in front of the hearth to spin the bottle. Katie John's heart pounded as the bottle whirled around and stopped, pointing more or less toward Howard.

"All right, Howard, Truth or Dare?" Jason said, businesslike.

"Oh geez! Uh—Truth."

Priscilla sat up, smiling at the bulky boy.

"Okay. Let's see." Jason glanced around at the kids, and Katie John thought he looked masterful. "All right, Bunch, did you ever steal anything, and if so, what? Tell the truth!"

Priscilla looked disappointed in the question, and Howard looked embarrassed.

"Well, actually, I never stole much," he confessed. "But one time when I was a little kid, in a drugstore I stuffed a handful of bubble gum in my pocket."

"Bubble gum!" The kids laughed.

"Yeah, it was really dumb." Howard was laughing, too, and shamefaced. "Because my pocket had a big hole in it, and the bubble gum scattered all over the floor. Everybody looked at me, and I had to go apologize to the clerk."

"Whoo!" the boys laughed and jeered. "Bubble Gum Bunch!"

"I'll punch whoever calls me that!" Howard punched after one of the guys.

"Next!" Trish called over the hullabaloo.

Chuck was the next spinner, and the bottle pointed to one of the eighth-grade cheerleaders. She chose Truth, too.

"Okay, who do you like—which boy?"

"You!"

"Nah, c'mon, tell the truth."

"It's the truth," she laughed. "I do like you. You didn't ask which boy I like *best.*"

"Ahhh!" Chuck went back to his seat, while everybody laughed.

"Next!"

Katie John shoved her plate behind her and watched the spinning bottle in horrible fascination. The game progressed from Truth and "Who do you like best?" to Dares and kissing.

Priscilla, bottle-spinner, said to Lou Bee, bottle-ee, "I dare you to kiss the boy you like the best."

Lou Bee cocked her head and giggled, while the boys whooped "Oo-hooo!" and Priscilla urged, "Now come on, sugar!"

Lou Bee's eyes sparkled. "All right, I'll give back the kiss you gave me." She went over to Ramon and kissed him on the mouth.

"Whooo!" the kids whooped and laughed. Ramon grinned.

Katie John swallowed. She thought Lou Bee was bold, yet she had to admire the easy way Lou Bee and Ramon laughed together, not embarrassed. She glanced over at Jason. He was just leaning back in his chair, a slight smile on his mouth, not whooping it up.

Oh, how she wished the bottle would point to him, so she could see what he'd do! No, she dreaded it.

And what would she do, if the bottle pointed to her? Sometimes it pointed to the same person twice, and then that person was skipped over, so eventually a turn could come to her.

There were more kisses—a cheerleader, a kazoo-band girl, two eighth-grade boys—more girls eligible for the Kissed Club.

Howard Bunch was next in front of the hearth with the bottle. "Okay, the bottle she spins," he chuckled. But he gave only a slight twist to the bottle so that it turned to point at Katie John.

"No fair!" she protested. "You didn't really spin it."

"No, come on, Katie!" some of the kids insisted. "Your turn, Katie John!"

"Truth or Dare?" Howard demanded, grinning at her.

She thought fast. If she took Truth, he might ask which boy she liked best.

"Dare."

"Okay, Katie John Tucker, I dare you to kiss one of these here boys!"

"You would!"

What to do? She could go over to her old buddy, shove up his sleeve and kiss Howard on the elbow. Everybody would laugh, and she'd be the usual Katie-clown. But she wasn't going to have her first real kiss in front of everybody. She didn't dare look at Jason.

"Come on, Katie John! Kissy-kissy!"

She got up and stepped over to Ramon. "Here's another one," she said, kissing him on the cheek. He smiled up at her in surprise.

"Hey, no fair!" the calls came. "Chicken!"

Lou Bee said sharply, "But you're still not kissed, yourself. You still can't wear the Kissed Club badge."

"That's right!" Katie John smiled with determination.

She moved on behind the circle, and at the same time Trish went to spin the bottle, and Jason got up abruptly. Katie didn't want to see what happened next. It was almost time for Dad to pick her up.

She'd just look outside, and if he was waiting, she'd say, "Thanks for a nice party," and get away.

The lamplit driveway was empty, but Katie lingered outside. She'd stayed through her turn in the stupid game; she didn't have to go back. Night air stirred in the oak trees around the house and made the leaves rustle. She shouldn't have come in the first place. She didn't know any more than she had before whether Jason liked Trish best or herself—or anybody.

Car lights approached along the road, then went on past. An oak leaf drifted off a tree, floated indecisively and settled on the ground.

Actually, the way Jason kept to himself, he wasn't much fun at a party.

"That's a kiddish game," Jason said behind her on the doorstep.

Katie whirled. "Uh—yes." Had he deliberately come out to be with her? "I was just looking to see if my dad had come." She looked again toward the road, and her earrings swung.

"Nice earrings." Jason touched one. "They shine in this lamplight."

Katie John felt a quiver that was both delightful and scary. She smiled at him, speechless.

Jason strolled a few steps, saying back, "That Ramon looked surprised for you to kiss him. Lou Bee, too!"

"Oh—it's just a game," Katie said, following him. She was pleased at how sophisticated she sounded.

131

"So say"—Jason looked around at her—"I need to get home early. Can I catch a ride down with you and your old man?"

Katie couldn't help beaming. "Certainly!"

The evening was retrieved. Jason had chosen to leave the party with her. She and Jason could tell Trish good-bye together!

9

Halloween at Wuthering Heights

The house was like a quiet tower for studying, as Katie John sat at her desk with her English assignment. Silence seemed to sift down through the house, colored only by slight sounds: the wheezes of Heavenly Spot, who slept on the floor by Katie's feet; an occasional clink of dishes in the kitchen below her room; the sigh of wind in the crack of the French doors that opened onto a small balcony.

Nevertheless, Katie was having trouble getting to work. She was supposed to write a description, and she couldn't think what to describe. Maybe the geodes?

A louder hum of wind sounded at the French doors. It was a drafty old house, and soon Dad would put a big storm window over the glass doors for the winter. Katie John was always a little sorry when the time came to be sealed in. A faint whistle of wind seeped from the china horn on the wall by her desk. It was the mouthpiece for an ancient speaking-tube system in the walls of the house, seldom used anymore except for fun at Halloween parties.

Fancifully, Katie John got up and said, "Hello?" into the china piece, but the house didn't answer. Only the wind moaned louder in the crack of the doors. Maybe she ought to write a description of the wind, Katie thought. She opened the French doors and stepped out onto her little balcony.

Oh, yes! Against the dark sky, wind tossed the top branches of the great mulberry tree that grew from the back yard down the steep hill; wind swirled her hair; gusts of wind wuthered around the corners of the brick house.

"Wuthering Heights!" Katie John exclaimed. "That's what this place is! Tonight it's Wuthering Heights!"

Such an eerie-sounding name ... The wind almost always blew on Halloween, too. . . . And then the chips of an idea came together in a glorious whole: Why not a party featuring "Halloween at Wuthering Heights"!

And she'd invite Jason.

Standing in the wind, Katie John thrilled to the idea. Yes, she wanted Jason to come to her house. There, on her own ground, how would he act toward her?

Riding in the car with him had seemed personal, even though he hadn't said much or done anything.

After Jason had gotten out, Dad had grumped, "You two were awfully close in that backseat."

She'd protested, "It's a *little* backseat!" But they had been as close as the time in the balloon basket.

Katie John went back into her room and shut out most of the wind. It wouldn't be a dull, stand-around party like Trish's was until they played that crazy game. No, *her* party would have lots of Halloween-type things to do, and Jason wouldn't have any chance to drift around on the edges.

An insistent howl sounded through the crack.

"Yes, all right!" Katie said, laughing. "You first, then—"

Quickly, while her impressions were fresh, she dashed off a colorful description of the wind around the house. Then she planned the party—what they could do, what they'd eat, what she would wear. Of course, it would be a costume party. And she would be . . . a gypsy! Last Halloween she had thought of being a gypsy fortune-teller, after having seen one at the Street Fair, but instead she had dressed as a black ghost. This year, for a new reason, she would be a gypsy.

She would invite Edwin, naturally. Katie John felt a moment's uneasiness. Jason and Edwin at the same party? But she couldn't leave Edwin out. And Sue, Bob, Howard— She smiled at herself, remembering how last year she'd tried so hard to keep boys

135

away from her Halloween party.

The next day at breakfast, however, Dad made a fuss about her having a boy-girl party.

"Not on Halloween night," he declared, "because I can't be here. That night I'm giving a talk for the Mystery Writers' Club in St. Louis. All about my favorite detective, snoopy young Annie Pete," he coaxed.

Katie John didn't think the girl in Dad's books was anything like herself, and she wasn't going to be coaxed out of it.

"It has to be on Halloween night," she insisted. "Otherwise, there's no point to it! You don't have to be here."

She felt a little guilty after she said that. It sounded as if she didn't want him at the party. Dad was the one she'd always joked with, for her mother was more serious and practical; he was the one with interesting ideas. Still, he'd be kind of in the way at the party, anyway.

But Dad was insisting, too. "If you're having boys, I need to keep an eye on things. They might get rowdy."

"Oh, Hugh, we can handle it," her mother said.

"You can't be everywhere. There are too many dark corners in this house." Dad shoved away his half-empty plate of eggs. "Abby, you didn't see how close Katie and that boy sat in the backseat."

Katie shifted on her chair. "Oh, Dad, it isn't as if we'll pair off at the party, or anything."

"It's the *anything* that worries me." Dad sat back, arms folded across his chest. Amazingly, it seemed he could not be coaxed or budged.

Katie John got up from the table, complaining bitterly. "Well, I think it's just rotten, when this house is so perfect for Halloween parties. How you can call Edwin Jones rowdy!"

Dad uncrossed his arms. "Hmph. I'm glad you haven't forgotten poor old Edwin."

"He isn't *poor old Edwin!*" Lou Bee was quite capable of entertaining both Edwin and Ramon at the party.

Katie John went to school kicking leaves. In Homemaking class Jason was as politely distant as ever. And Edwin wasn't even in the lunchroom at noon. Rather to Katie's surprise, not one Kissed Club badge appeared on a girl's chest. Monday, after Trish's party, a few new badges had been sported, but Trish hadn't worn hers, and now the badges had disappeared like dew on the grass in the morning sun.

When Katie got home from school, she found that her mother had won Dad over about the Halloween party. He had been mollified by the shot about Edwin, and he had agreed when Abby said Sue's mother would help her keep an eye on the kids.

"Oh, thanks, Dad!" Katie John hugged him. "We'll be good! Pretty good."

"Be gooder than good," her father called after her, only half smiling.

137

But Katie was already rushing up the stairs to her room to start lettering invitations on notepaper:

You Are Invited to
Halloween at Wuthering Heights

Jason, she addressed an invitation, *Sue*—not too large a group. She didn't want a whole horde of kids, like at Trish's party. Oh, goodness. Katie John threw down her pen and sat back, mouth tight. Having just been to a party at Trish's house, she couldn't very well leave her out. Hoping against hope that Trish wouldn't come, Katie made an invitation for her.

So, besides Jason, Edwin, Sue, Bob and Trish, she'd ask Priscilla, Howard, Lou Bee, Ramon and— Oh, what about Delby Hitchens, downstairs? She couldn't very well have a party rampaging all over the house and not invite him.

As if summoned by her thought, Delby appeared at her bedroom door.

"Hey, Katie, c'n I come in? I got somethin' to tell ya."

How had he found her room in all that house? "What?"

Delby flopped on Katie's bed. "I'm shakin' it off, cuttin' out."

"Huh?"

"Can't stand the stuck-up kids in your snotty school anymore. I'm leaving."

Delby looked belligerent, and Katie John had the

138

feeling he thought she was stuck-up, too.

"Delby, I don't think you should be in Katie's room," said Mother, coming in the door. She looked askance at the boy lounging on the bed.

Delby sat up. "It's all right, Mrs. T. I just came up to tell Katie I'm leaving. Goin' back down to Joeville, where people like me."

"Why, we like you," Katie John said, feeling guilty. "It takes time to get acquainted."

"Ain't got that much time," Delby said. He stood up. "I'll be goin' on home this weekend."

So he'd be gone by the time of the party next Tuesday.

Ashamed, Katie said, "Well, it's been fun knowing you. I—" Her mother had stepped back out into the hallway. "Delby, I'm sorry. I—I'm just not old enough for you."

"Sure, kid." He tousled her head as he went out.

And she never would be!

Before finishing the invitations, Katie John phoned Sue to talk about the party. Upon consultation, Betsy Ann and Pete Hallstrom were added to the list. Sue pointed out that Jason Schreiber was the only eighth-grader, but Katie John set her mouth against inviting Chuck. With Chuck there, Jason might stick with him all the time. Next morning Katie and Sue went to school early and taped the invitations to the kids' lockers.

As the hallway began to fill with people, Katie John lingered near her locker and watched Jason's down the way, to make sure nobody ripped off his invitation before he got there.

Howard Bunch came clattering down the hall. "Hey, I can come, but what's this mean, 'Wuthering Heights'?"

"That's what I'm calling my house for that night. See, *wuthering* means, well, probably it's the sound the wind makes, moaning around, and you know my house is on a hill—*heights.*"

"Huh. Scary. Okay, I'll be there." Howard bounded away.

Other people came up asking the same question, and Katie John realized that none of the kids had heard of the book *Wuthering Heights.*

Except for Edwin. "It's that book you said you read last summer." He looked at her, his eyes narrowed. "It really got to you, didn't it? Anyway, I'm glad you're finally going to let us guys come to one of your parties."

Katie watched him suspiciously, but his face was innocent enough. "Yes"—she nodded—"time enough. And look, Edwin," she thought aloud suddenly, "I've got a job for you at the party, so try to get there early."

She'd planned to ask Sue to do it, but Edwin could do it a lot better.

"What is it?"

Katie John grinned. "Halloween surprise. I'll tell you when you get there."

At last Jason arrived at his locker and studied the

140

invitation. Katie made herself busy getting something out of her locker. When Jason came sauntering down the hall with the note in his hand, her heart thumped hard.

"When's Halloween?" he asked. "The thirtieth or the thirty-first?"

"Good grief!" How anybody wouldn't know when Halloween was! "The thirty-first. Next Tuesday."

"Oh, yeah. Well, I guess I can come. Thanks." His speckled blue eyes flashed at her, then looked down at the invitation again.

Katie John waited for a count of *one, two,* and sure enough, it came.

"What is 'Wuthering Heights'?"

"My house." Patiently, Katie explained again what *wuthering* meant. She felt sad, because he didn't even know he was like Heathcliff. "Have you ever heard of Heathcliff?" she asked.

"Uh—let's see. Wasn't that a cat in a comic strip?"

Katie sighed. "Maybe so."

She moved away toward class. He couldn't help it if he hadn't read the book, she told herself. It didn't matter.

But she felt deflated about the party. Maybe the whole thing would be a bust.

Over the weekend, however, her enthusiasm revived as she and Sue prepared for Halloween. They baked cookies and made jack-o'-lantern faces on them with orange icing. They stored jugs of apple cider in the fruit cellar to chill. They carved a crop of pumpkins into weird faces, equipped them with candles and populated the old house with them: two on the front porch, one on the refreshment table in the back parlor, and the rest in dark corners of the house. Sue's lower lip got pouty when Katie John wouldn't tell her what they were going to do at the party; but she cheered up helping to make a dummy of a headless woman.

The night of the party the wind blew on cue, and the few renters were bribed with cookies to be patient about the kids swarming over the house. Between the times she answered the doorbell for early trick-or-treaters, Katie John toured the house to make sure everything was in place and all the pumpkin candles were lit. The main secret she'd been keeping from Sue was that they were going to have a treasure hunt through the house. All the clues were planted and the prizes hidden at the goal, inside the hinged back steps. The first team to open the correct tricky step would find bags of gold-covered chocolate coins. The second team would get a sack of black licorice whips.

Katie John stood in the hallway at the bottom of the stairwell, listening to the last quiet of the house before the eruption of the party. She could hear the wind wuthering outside.

"You good old house, you're just made for Halloween!"

While her mother took care of trick-or-treaters,

Katie went up to her room to transform herself into a romantic gypsy, a being possibly as enchanting as Catherine Earnshaw. She turned on the one green light bulb she'd inserted in her bedlamp and grinned at the headless woman lying on her bed.

"Hi, honey!"

In the dim green light the dummy looked horribly real, with red ketchup smearing out at the neck. One of the clues was hidden under the plastic cloth that caught the ketchup.

"Gory!" Katie laughed, shucking her clothes.

From the closet she took her favorite embroidered blouse and the swishy ankle-length skirt Mother had made for the gypsy costume. Her stomach gurgled as she put on the low-cut blouse. She thought it was because of the sight on her bed. But her innards grew more and more queasy as she dressed. She went to the bathroom. She came back and fussed with her hair until she got the kerchief knotted right, with some hair showing, and then she inserted the long gold earrings. Turning her head in front of the mirror, she surveyed gypsy-Katie. What would Jason think of the way she looked? She went to the bathroom again.

The doorbell rang, and this time it was party-comers. Running down the front stairs, Katie saw Mrs. Halsey and Sue, who looked perfect as a fairy godmother, complete with wand starred on the tip. Trish Hardwicke arrived right behind them. She wasn't wearing a costume. Her clothes were so smart, however, that Katie John felt frumpy in her gypsy outfit.

"You're right about one thing," Trish said, "the wind certainly does blow on this hill. It's blown out the candles in your pumpkins on the porch."

"Oh!" Katie hurried to find matches.

"What an *interesting* old house," Trish said in her most sophisticated voice, eyeing the clutter of antique vases in the parlor. "And this rug—it must be very old."

She toed the worn spot in a small Oriental rug that was frayed at the edge.

"Yes."

Katie rushed outside with the matches. She could strangle Trish! Her matches kept going out in the gusts of wind, but fortunately, Edwin arrived and got the pumpkins lit again.

"Oh, Edwin, you look just great!"

Wearing a long black coat and carrying a short broom, Edwin was a chimney sweep. Somewhere he'd found a tall, battered black hat, and he'd smeared his face with soot. He grinned through the soot.

"You look good, too. You going to tell fortunes?"

"No, you are! Come on."

Through the wind, chill off the river, she led Edwin around to the side porch and smuggled him up the back stairs to her bedroom.

"Oh, gol, Katie John!" Edwin exclaimed at the sight of the headless woman on the bed. "That's the

144

most— How did you—"

"Never mind that right now." She pointed him to the china horn on the wall by her desk. "You know about the speaking-tube system. Okay, as the kids arrive, they can ask a question at the speaker in the parlor, and you answer up here. Make your voice all spooky and give some weird answer. Okay?"

Edwin regarded the china piece. "I'm not good at thinking of weird things. But"—his smile flashed white in the soot—"okay, I'll try."

Katie John hurried downstairs, her earrings swaying. Sue, Trish and the two mothers were just standing around.

"Now, the first thing we'll do—" Katie began.

The doorbell rang. Priscilla, Betsy Ann, Howard and Pete were standing on the porch. None of them were wearing costumes, except for Bob, coming up the walk behind them. Bob had on a flouncy old-woman dress with his pants legs sticking out below.

"Oh, Katie John, you look so cute," Priscilla said, coming in. Kindly she explained to the others, "Katie can change right here to go on to the movie, but we can't."

"Huh?" Katie goggled at them. "Movie?"

"Sure!" Howard said. "Can't miss the midnight show. Everybody's going."

"Yes," Priscilla said. "Of course, it won't break up your party, sugar, because the show doesn't start until ten-thirty."

"Oh. Well—"

Everybody stood around in the parlor. Katie John worked to get them moving.

"Listen, everybody," she called over the chatter, "the Great Hoodoo is here! Out of the dark, the Hoodoo will speak!"

"Huh? Who-do?" Giggles.

"The Great Hoodoo will answer your questions! Ask your deepest questions"—Katie John made her voice hollow—"at the hole to the Beyond." She pointed to the china horn on the wall by the fireplace.

"Oh, yes, it's an old speaking-tube system," Priscilla said to Trish. "Remember, Betsy Ann, last year?"

Katie John glared at Priscilla. "I'll show you how to question the Great Hoodoo."

She blew into the mouthpiece. There was a long pause, and Trish began to talk to Pete. Katie John wondered if Edwin remembered he had to move the metal lever in order to be heard. She blew again.

At last, "Yess?" whispered through the tubes.

"Oh, Great Hoodoo," Katie called into the mouthpiece, "tell me—uh—which ghosts will walk in the graveyard tonight?"

She put her ear close to the mouthpiece and heard an eerie moan, then, "On-ly the ghost of the Unknown Soldier will walk tonight—ohhhh."

Edwin was too serious to play-act in front of peo-

146

ple, but he was perfectly dramatic when he could be concealed.

"Thank you!" Katie laughed into the mouthpiece. "All right," she said to the others, "try out the Great Hoodoo."

"Trust Katie John!" Howard jumped to be first at the china horn. "Okay, Hoodoo, what's your real name?"

The others stupidly got in a line behind him.

"Look, some of you could be getting cider and cookies." Katie pointed through the open sliding doors to the refreshment table in the back parlor.

The doorbell rang. The people on the porch were Ramon and Lou Bee. They weren't wearing costumes. Greeting them, Katie John looked out into the windy darkness. Where was Jason? Wasn't he going to come?

Anyway, there were shrieks of laughter in the parlor, and the kids were moving around more. The doorbell rang again, not Jason but a little white-sheeted ghost. Katie handed him a cookie, and then the front walk was empty.

Everybody had had a turn at the speaking tube. She couldn't make Edwin stay up there forever. Katie went to the china piece and called, "Oh, Hoodoo, are you willing to show yourself? Will you descend on us now?"

"I will come," answered the sepulchral voice.

147

When slow thumps sounded on the stairs, the kids pushed into the front hall to see who the Hoodoo was. Edwin made his descent dramatically at first, but then he laughed in embarrassment and ran on down the steps. At the same time, the doorbell rang. Trish, who was nearest, opened the door.

"Well, it's about time," she said to Jason.

"Sorry I'm late," he said, just as if Trish were the hostess. He was wearing his regular clothes.

Katie John was caught in the push of kids back into the parlor, and she couldn't even say hello to Jason.

Sue whispered to her, "I feel silly in this fairy godmother costume, when hardly anybody's dressed up."

Howard was teasing Edwin, and Katie John told Edwin how scary he'd been. She finally did get to speak to Jason, but it was a nothing kind of situation. He just said hi, helping himself to cider, and he didn't say anything about how she looked.

Katie John took him over to a window. "Listen. Hear the wuthering?"

"Uh-hunh." He nodded. "Really windy."

He sipped his cider and glanced around the shadowy back parlor, its walls lined with oval-framed portraits of ancestors. Gilt had broken off some of the frames, and Great-Grandfather Clark's picture was water stained from the time the plumbing had leaked from above. Katie hadn't realized how shabby the back parlor looked.

148

Everybody was standing around again.

Katie John took a big breath. "Okay, everybody, now for the main event! A treasure hunt!"

She explained it to them, and they numbered off for two teams, each with a different trail of clues. Trish and Jason were on the same team.

She heard Jason reading off the first clue, "High above, the headless woman speaks, under her—yuck!—under her blood."

"How disgusting!" Trish exclaimed.

"Shee." Jason shook his head. "I feel like a little kid."

Oh! Katie felt sudden tears in her eyes. He didn't have to act so— Since she couldn't help solve the clues, having made them up, she had planned to follow first one team, then another, to be in on the fun. But now—

Jason's troop started up the stairs, while Sue and Edwin led the other team toward the dining room, following the clue *At last the dumb waiter speaks.* Katie John trailed behind Sue's group. Moving around the house, the two teams kept passing each other. Howard and some of the kids got caught up in the fun of a treasure chase, but Jason seemed more bewildered about it than anything. In the third-floor hallway, he caught Katie's arm.

"What does this clue mean? I don't get it. I mean, you know your house, but we don't."

"We went in a renter's room by mistake," Trish said. "It was so embarrassing. Some old man— I

149

really don't think a treasure hunt is quite the thing in a rooming house."

Curtly, Katie John interpreted the clue. She watched Jason and Trish go down the stairs together, ahead of Lou Bee and the others on their team. At Wuthering Heights, Heathcliff had always sided with Catherine against everyone else.

Just then Heavenly Spot came bounding up the stairs to join the fun, and Lou Bee stumbled on the dog. "Careful!" Jason caught her. Katie saw him look at Lou Bee in that long special way. What on earth?

Sue's team found the treasure first, without any tips from Katie. "Wow, steps that open up! Gold!" Howard and Ramon began to explore the other hinged steps. "What a tricky place to keep hammers and things!" To relieve the crush on the lower stairs, Katie John sat on a step higher up. So she saw Trish and Jason come into the pumpkin-lit hallway above.

"Up and down, up and down—I feel like I'm a hamster on an exercise wheel!" Trish laughed.

Katie saw Jason look at Trish in that special way. "Oh, well, it's just a kid party," he said with that slight smile.

He was so—cool! That's all he tried to be, Katie John thought in a rage. The way he looked at a girl—it wasn't special, if he looked at every girl that way!

Coming on down the darkened stairs, Jason saw Katie. He said, "The last clue tells something about

'Look in the stairs.' Are you the prize?"

"Not at all!"

Katie pushed on down the stairs through the kids and watched Jason and his team find the licorice whips and laugh over them. It was too early to break up the party. Her mother hadn't even set out the hot pumpkin tarts on the table yet.

"Okay," she said grimly, "we've got one more scary thing to do. Come on, everybody."

Katie John led the way to the cellar stairs. Telling ghost stories in the fruit cellar was to have been the climax of the party. Now, with Jason and Trish acting so superior, probably the storytelling would be a flop, but she didn't know what else to do with the kids until it was decently time for them to leave.

She felt shriveled. She wasn't a romantic gypsy. Bringing Jason into her house hadn't transformed him into a faithful friend. Jason didn't fit in Wuthering Heights, because he wasn't really like Heathcliff. She'd just tried to believe he was. She'd just dreamed it all up in her stupid mind.

As she opened the door to the fruit cellar, she could take no pleasure in the dank smell of oldness, because she could imagine how it would smell to Trish. Inside, a lit pumpkin grinned from the top of a wooden icebox, and there were old benches she'd lugged in from the barn, so they wouldn't have to sit on the cold brick floor. Katie John plopped down on a bench. Probably Trish and Jason would think it was a junky place to be.

151

As the others came in, Sue squealed, "Ooo, it's a dungeon!" trying to contribute to the spookiness. And Howard made menacing lunges at each person coming in the door. Lou Bee seemed really impressed.

"You've got more *places* in this house!"

Katie John only huddled on the bench, waiting for Trish and Jason to come in and raise their eyebrows— Suddenly she straightened up. What was she doing, sitting there being ashamed of her own beloved fruit cellar? And where were Jason and Trish? And Edwin.

She went out and saw them across the basement, standing at the open door of the Hitchens apartment, where light and TV sound poured out.

Mrs. Hitchens called, "Just wanted to see the kids all dressed up. This guy looks good." She pointed to Edwin. "Lemme see you."

Katie went over to show herself, and Jason and Trish moved toward the fruit cellar. When she and Edwin came away, the kids were squealing inside, but Trish and Jason were still lingering in the doorway, and she heard what they said.

"—messy apartment. Did you ever see such a tacky old house?"

"Yeah," Jason muttered. "I'm surprised Katie John would want to show it off at a party."

"Tacky! I guess you—" Katie's voice broke.

"Say, this is a noble old house!" Edwin shoved his broom at Jason's chest. "It's a lot more interesting than that modern chicken coop you live in!"

Jason pushed the broom back, and Edwin squared away to fight.

"Oh, Edwin," Trish said, making it light, "you live in a cemetery, so naturally you'd like a dismal old house. You and Katie are two of a kind."

Katie John's chin went up. "Yes, we are! And glad of it! I love this old house, and anybody who doesn't like it can—can just leave!"

"Oh, don't be such a baby. However," Trish said to Jason, "probably we should go early, not to stand in line for popcorn at the movie."

So they'd had a date, all along. Katie John felt a pang. And yet, did she really care? She looked at Jason, who only shrugged a little. Even now he didn't have anything worthwhile to say. How could such a good-looking boy be so dull?

"Okay, 'bye, guys. Come on, Edwin, let's go tell ghost stories."

Jason and Trish said what a swell party it was and headed for the basement stairs, but Edwin didn't move toward the fruit cellar right away.

He said, "Katie John, would you like to see what a cemetery is like on Halloween?"

"Hey! Yes!"

"Good, then why don't you walk me home, after the party, and we'll check it out." Edwin looked so strange in that high black hat, with soot all over his face. "My dad said he'd drive you home."

"You mean you've already asked him?"

153

"Yeah, but I waited to say anything about it until I saw how you—I mean, how it was with—" He glanced toward the cellar stairs, where Jason and Trish could be heard thumping up the hollow wooden steps.

' "Oh, Edwin, you should know—"

Exploring a Halloween graveyard . . . The ghost of the Unknown Soldier wafting over the rows of white markers . . . Maybe teenagers would be carousing through the cemetery and kissing under the Black Angel monument. Or maybe the cemetery would be quiet, all the graves peacefully sleeping. Whatever it was like on Halloween night, it would be fascinating to find out. To find out with Edwin.

In the properly spooky fruit cellar, Howard was telling a story in a properly spooky voice, "Step . . . step . . ."

Yes, ghost stories in a dungeon in a good old house were right for Halloween, not looking at a movie. She knew that, and she was sorry Jason didn't. But Edwin did.

He touched her arm. "I'll bet there's never been a gypsy in that cemetery," he said, "not like you."

Katie John smiled at him, feeling the earrings dripping from her ears. Then she gave him a whole-hearted grin. With Edwin she didn't feel childish or clownish, but only eager to see where herself would take her.

"And never a loyal chimney sweep like you," she said.